SECOND CHANCE

LAURA SCOTT

READSCAPE PUBLISHING, LLC

SECOND CHANCE

by

Laura Scott

SECOND CHANCE

CRYSTAL LAKE SERIES (IN ORDER)

Healing Her Heart
A Soldier's Promise
Coming Home
Worth The Wait
Christmas Reunion
Second Chance

Love Inspired Suspense Books

Wrongly Accused (SWAT Series)
Down To The Wire (SWAT Series)
Under The Lawman's Protection (SWAT Series)
Forgotten Memories (SWAT Series)
Holiday On The Run (SWAT Series)
Mirror Image (SWAT Series)
Shielding His Christmas Witness (Callahan Confidential)
The Only Witness (Callahan Confidential)
Christmas Amnesia (Callahan Confidential)
Shattered Lullaby (Callahan Confidential)

Primary Suspect (Callahan Confidential)
Protecting His Secret Son (Callahan Confidential)

1

Sheriff's deputy, Devon Armbruster, half-carried half-dragged the highly intoxicated Jimmy Campbell into the ER of Hope County Hospital. This was the third time in the past eighteen months that he'd pulled Jimmy over for driving without a valid license and driving under the influence.

"Gotta get home," Jimmy mumbled as he tripped, and would have fallen flat on his face, if Dev hadn't been hanging onto him. "Sally's gonna be mad."

Yeah, that was a massive understatement. Especially since Jimmy wasn't going home anytime soon. He was going to spend time in jail, and considering this was Jimmy's third offense, he was looking at a good six to twelve months behind bars.

Devon held onto his temper with an effort. After losing his fiancée to a drunk driving accident five years ago, he didn't have a lot of patience for Jimmy's plight. Although Dev was glad he'd pulled Jimmy over before he'd hurt anyone unlike the person that had taken his fiancée's life.

Dev shook off the flash of anger and helped Jimmy over to the desk.

"We're here for a legal blood draw," Dev said to Eve, one of the ER nurses who glanced over when they walked in.

"Take room three," she said with a wave of her hand. "I'll be right over."

"Can I call Sally? Please?" Jimmy asked, slurring his words. "Gotta tell her I'm sorry."

"Not yet, but soon," Dev promised.

Thankfully Jimmy wasn't an angry or belligerent drunk, so Devon didn't need back-up to get the legal blood work that would prove what he already knew, that Jimmy was well beyond the legal limit.

It was frustrating to arrest the same people over and over again. As much as he'd enjoyed living in the small town of Crystal Lake, Wisconsin, lately he didn't feel as if he was making enough of an impact here.

Not compared to his older brother, Steve Armbruster, who had assisted in breaking up some serious crime rings in Milwaukee, before he'd lost his battle with pancreatic cancer.

What would be Dev's legacy? Nothing close to his big brother's, that was for sure. His brother's death six months ago had spurred him into action. He'd applied for jobs within several big city police departments.

So far, no one had called to follow up on the applications he'd submitted in both Madison and Milwaukee. Maybe he'd have to go out a little farther, for example the Twin Cities. He'd rather avoid Chicago, but maybe he was being too picky.

Shaking off his maudlin thoughts, Dev tried to focus on the issue at hand. Eve came and drew Jimmy's blood, putting the vial in the chain of custody kit so it could be submitted as legal evidence.

"No problem."

Dev looked down at Jimmy who was slumped over in his seat, snoring loudly. Obviously, getting him outside and into the back seat of his squad wouldn't be easy.

"Help! Please, help!"

Dev glanced over in surprise to find Janelle Larson, one of the ER nurses, dressed in street clothes, and rushing into the arena holding a young blond haired boy in her arms. "Sebastian is running a fever of a hundred point four despite acetaminophen."

Dev frowned, wondering what was going on. He'd always had a soft spot for Janelle, especially after the way she'd taken care of him two years ago when he'd been shot in the line of duty. There wasn't anything but friendship between them though, since she'd been seeing some guy, whose name escaped him at the moment. Larry? Lance? Something like that.

Dev quickly cuffed Jimmy to the chair, just to be sure he didn't try to leave on his own, and then followed Janelle. Not to intrude, but to offer support if needed.

"Let's get him into a room," Merry Crain, one of the ER nurses said in a calm, soothing voice. "Dr. Gabe is here, and will be in soon."

"I'm Sebastian's legal guardian. He has kidney failure and receives peritoneal dialysis three times a day," Janelle said, a worried frown furrowing her brow. "I'm afraid his catheter site might be infected."

"Let me get a quick set of vital signs, okay?"

Janelle nodded and moved to the side so that Merry could examine the boy. Dev stepped up beside her.

"Hey, are you alright?" he asked in a low voice. "Is there something I can do to help?"

Janelle swung around to look at him, her eyes bright with tears. "Hi Devon, thanks for the offer. Sebastian has already gone through so much, more than any four-year old should have to endure. I can't bear the thought of anything happening to him."

"Try not to worry, you know better than anyone the staff here will take good care of him. Isn't Sebastian your sister's son? When did you become his legal guardian?"

Janelle swiped away her tears and shrugged. "Since Lisa died three weeks ago. Sebastian's father lost his parental rights about a year after he was born, and I have to say I'm glad he's been locked up in jail."

His heart squeezed in sympathy. "So of course you stepped up to take the little guy."

She sniffled and nodded. "The state social workers were so glad, because I'm a nurse and wasn't put off by his medical issues. It's been a steep learning curve, but so far we're hanging in there."

Dev couldn't imagine what it must be like to become a mother overnight, not to mention for a child with medical needs. For a moment the night he'd lost Debra flashed in his mind. She'd been pregnant when she was killed in the head-on collision. In fact, if the baby had survived, the child would be close to the same age as Sebastian.

He swallowed hard and pushed the painful memories away. This wasn't about him, but about Janelle. And he owed her for saving his life. "Are you sure there's nothing I can do for you?" he asked. "Do you have someone helping you?"

Janelle flashed him a lopsided smile. "Thanks, I appreciate the offer. But we'll be fine."

The way she avoided his direct gaze gave him the impression there was something she wasn't saying. "Why are you here alone? Where's your boyfriend?"

She lifted a shoulder in a careless shrug. "Lane wasn't interested in sticking around once he knew that I was taking custody of Sebastian. Which is fine with me, things weren't all that great between us anyway. Sebastian and I are better off without him."

Dev reined in a flash of anger. No doubt she was better off without the idiot, but still, talk about being cold and callous. Turning your back on a sick four-year old? What was up with that?

Before he could say anything more, Dr. Gabe Allen came into the room. Dev backed off so that Janelle could participate in the conversation about the boy's medical care.

"We'll send a culture from the peritoneal catheter site, give him another dose of acetaminophen, and then start some IV antibiotics," Gabe said. "I'd like to keep him here in the hospital overnight so that we can watch him closely for the next twenty-four hours."

Janelle nodded. "Okay, but I plan to stay here with him."

"Of course, that's no problem," Gabe assured her.

Dev watched as Janelle moved closer to Sebastian, bending over the side rail of the gurney to talk to him in a low reassuring tone. With Sebastian's blond hair the exact same shade as Janelle's, they looked enough alike to make the average person think they were mother and son, instead of aunt and nephew.

Glancing at his watch, Dev was glad to see the time was almost eleven-thirty at night, which meant his shift was just about over. He'd drive Jimmy to jail, then maybe come back, see if there was anything more he could do for Janelle and Sebastian.

Just as friends. Despite the fact that Janelle wasn't seeing that jerk of a boyfriend any more, Dev was in no position to get emotionally involved. There was more at stake than his plans to move to a big city police department.

Unfortunately, Janelle and Sebastian were a painful reminder of everything he'd loved and lost.

JANELLE CAUGHT a glimpse of Devon leaving the ER with an obviously intoxicated Jimmy Campbell. It had been nice of Dev to come over to offer support.

She closed her eyes for a moment, praying for strength. Leaning on God and faith would help her get through this. She loved Sebastian very much, but that fact alone hadn't made the transition of becoming a mother overnight any easier.

For the first few days, Sebastian kept asking about his mommy, and no matter how many times she explained that his mommy was up in heaven, he didn't seem to grasp the concept. Finally she bought a stuffed angel and convinced him that his Mommy was an angel in heaven. Sebastian had calmed down after that, and slept with the angel every night. Janelle wasn't sure if the fact that he'd stopped asking about his mother was a good thing or not.

She bent down to press a kiss on his soft hair, breathing in the sweet scent of baby shampoo. He was such a good little boy, tolerating his peritoneal dialysis treatments better than she'd ever expected. Surely he'd pull through this latest threat without a problem.

When Merry returned to start Sebastian's IV, Janelle's stomach clenched at the realization she'd have to help hold him down. Funny how different it was to be on this side of the bed. Usually, she was the one urging parents to help hold their kids during medical treatments.

"Shh, Sebastian, it's okay. I'm here. It won't hurt for long," she whispered as Merry inserted the catheter.

Sebastian's crying ripped at her heart, making her eyes well in sympathy. She hated knowing that he had to suffer more pain on top of everything else.

"All done," Merry said cheerfully, once the catheter was in place and the IV fluids running.

"No more ouchies," Janelle murmured to Sebastian.

"Nana," he whispered, cuddling close.

She held him for a few minutes, until the trauma of being stuck with a needle passed. Sebastian used to call her Nanelle, but since she'd taken custody of him, he'd shortened it to Nana. She didn't mind in the least.

In fact, she hoped one day he might call her mama.

"Anything else?" Merry asked as she adjusted the rate of his IV fluids.

"No, but go easy on the fluids, remember he has kidney disease," Janelle warned.

"I haven't forgotten, but fluids are key to battling infection. We may opt to do an extra exchange if necessary."

Janelle bit her lip and nodded. Of course Gabe and Merry knew what they were doing. When had she become such a worry wart?

Since taking custody of Sebastian, she tried to tell herself to back off a bit, but then something like this happened, and she was right back to where she'd started. She was so afraid of doing something wrong, of failing as Sebastian's surrogate mother, the biggest, most important role of her life.

She couldn't stand the thought of anything bad happening to Sebastian. She loved him so much. In just three weeks she'd found she couldn't imagine her life without him.

After about fifteen minutes Sebastian finally drifted off to sleep. His forehead still felt too warm, but she hoped his fever would come down once the fluids and antibiotics kicked in.

She stroked a hand over his hair, then made sure the side-rails were locked on the gurney, before sinking into a chair and wearily rubbing her eyes. Sebastian had been fitful all day; she probably should have realized there was a problem sooner, but the catheter site had looked fine until the last exchange, right before bed. She'd never expected that the small amount of redness could become a raging infection so quickly. She was a nurse, but had needed to read up on kidney failure, to make sure she was well versed in Sebastian's treatment plan.

For some reason, she felt woefully inadequate to be Sebastian's guardian. She tried to tell herself that her nursing background was a bonus, and other foster parents couldn't provide the same care she could. At times like this, though, it was easy to have self-doubts. Especially since she still had a lot to learn about the nuances of Sebastian's kidney failure.

"Everything okay in here?" Merry asked in a whisper.

Janelle raised her head and forced a smile. "Sure, we're fine."

"Phoebe will be your nurse on the night shift," Merry whispered. "She'll be in shortly."

Janelle nodded, knowing they were in good hands. All the nurses in the hospital were great at their jobs. One of the things she enjoyed most about working here was the easy camaraderie amongst the staff, even the physicians. That hadn't been her experience at the large Madison hospital where she'd worked prior to moving to Crystal Lake.

Sebastian was on the kidney transplant list, which meant either moving back to Madison or enduring long commutes back and forth for treatment after his transplant. A problem she didn't want to think about at the moment.

Her stomach rumbled with hunger and she remembered she hadn't eaten much more than the low sodium soup she'd tried to get Sebastian to eat for dinner.

The cafeteria was closed for the night, though, so her only option was vending machine food; not the least bit appealing.

Sebastian moaned in his sleep, and she shot to her feet, crossing over to make sure he was all right. Was it her imagination or did his forehead feel a bit cooler?

She straightened out the IV tubing then bent over to brush a kiss across his temple, her heart aching for him. He had endured so much adversity in his short lifetime. She prayed again, this time for Sebastian to heal quickly and for the possibility of a kidney transplant, one he so desperately needed.

There was a soft tapping on the doorframe, causing her to glance over her shoulder. She'd expected Phoebe, but it was Devon who stood there dressed in casual clothes: well-worn blue jeans and a soft long sleeved T-shirt, instead of the brown uniform he'd worn earlier. He was handsome no matter what he wore, with his thick dark brown hair, broad shoulders, and deep brown eyes. Something she hadn't really noticed until just this minute.

A realization that caught her off guard.

What was wrong with her? Sebastian was fighting off a life-threatening infection and she was thinking about how handsome Devon looked. She should be ashamed of herself.

"Hungry?" he whispered, holding up the bag. "I brought enough for both of us."

Touched by his thoughtful generosity, she nodded. "Yes, but how did you know?"

He shrugged and gestured for her to come out of Sebastian's room. "I feel bad eating in front of him, maybe it's better if we head down to the cafeteria." His voice went up on the end, as if he were asking a question.

She hesitated, then shook her head. "How about the ER staff break room? That way I won't be too far away if Sebastian needs something."

"Sounds good." Devon smiled and gestured for her to lead the way toward the break-room.

As they passed by the central nurse's station, she caught a glimpse of Sebastian's night nurse, a pretty girl with dark hair and wide light gray eyes. "Hey, Phoebe, Sebastian is sleeping. I'll be in the back room if you need anything."

"Sounds good. We're working on getting him an inpatient bed. I'll let you know once we have one assigned."

"Thanks." Janelle darted around the nurse's station to the small break-room located in the back corner of the ER.

"Do you want the cheeseburger or the chicken sandwich?" Dev asked, when they were seated next to each other at the table.

She lifted a brow. "I'm fairly certain you want the cheeseburger, right?"

"I like them both," Devon said firmly. "Seriously, you pick."

"I'll take the chicken sandwich," she said.

"Are you sure?"

"Yes, I was just giving you a hard time." She picked up

the sandwich and silently thanked God for providing them with food, before taking a healthy bite. "Hmm, this is great. How did you know I was hungry?"

"I assumed that taking care of a sick kid would be time consuming and that you might not have remembered to eat dinner. Besides, I was hungry, too."

Janelle stared down at her sandwich for a minute, before raising her gaze to meet his. "It was nice of you to think about me, Devon," she said in a soft tone. She couldn't remember the last time anyone had done something nice for her. Certainly not Lane, since he'd always been primarily concerned with himself. Something that should have clued her in much sooner than it had.

"You're welcome," he responded lightly, although his intense gaze held hers for a long second.

Flustered, she pulled her gaze away and focused her attention on eating, knowing that she couldn't afford to read attraction into Devon's kind gesture. He was being a good friend, nothing more.

She didn't have time for anything else, even if she wanted to get involved in another relationship. Which she didn't.

Nothing was more important than Sebastian's health and well-being. Certainly not her personal life.

The little boy deserved every ounce of her attention, and then some. Maybe she hadn't helped as much as she should have while Lisa was still alive, but she was bound and determined to make up for her lapse in judgment now.

No matter what the cost, personally or professionally.

2

Devon tore his gaze from Janelle's, staring blankly down at his cheeseburger for a long moment. What was wrong with him? Why was he suddenly so acutely aware of Janelle?

And where on earth had that flash of sizzling attraction come from?

He gave himself a mental shake, trying to get things back on an even keel. He needed to stop thinking about how beautiful Janelle looked and concentrate on keeping her in the friend category."So how long do you think your nephew will have to stay in the hospital? Did Dr. Gabe give you any sort of timeline?"

Janelle let out a heavy sigh. "I'm not sure, I'm hoping he'll be able to kick this infection pretty quickly. But that might be simply wishful thinking since Gabe mentioned there is a possibility of Sebastian needing surgery."

"Surgery?" he echoed with a frown. "For what?"

"He has a catheter in his abdomen which is what I use to infuse his peritoneal dialysis solution. If the infection in the catheter site doesn't clear up, they may need to put in a new one."

"Poor little guy," Dev murmured. He wasn't an expert on medical issues, but obviously, the boy's condition was more serious than he'd realized.

"Yeah, I know." Janelle set her chicken sandwich down, as if she'd lost her appetite. "And if that happens, he might need to go on hemodiaylsls, which is something I can't provide for him at home. He's not having any significant problems as a result of his peritoneal dialysis, and I've heard the side effects are worse with hemodialysis. I guess at this point, all I can do is hope and pray he gets the opportunity for a kidney transplant, soon."

Devon glanced up in surprise, somehow he hadn't known that was an option. "I take it you're not a match?"

Janelle shook her head slowly. "No, although you have no idea how much I wish I were. Apparently he's blood type B negative, which is relatively rare, something he inherited from his father."

Devon scowled. "And his father won't donate?"

Janelle grimaced. "His father used to be an IV drug addict, so he's not eligible to donate. Which is fine, since I don't really want Sebastian to have anything to do with his father. I don't trust Grant one bit. He's in jail because he physically abused Lisa and Sebastian, then took all her money and valuables. I'm afraid if he gets out of jail, he'd only try to use the situation to his advantage."

Devon shook his head. Hard to believe how much little Sebastian had the deck stacked against him. "I'm sorry, Janelle. All of this must be tough to deal with."

She abruptly straightened in her seat and picked up her sandwich with determination. "I'm fine and so is Sebastian.

I firmly believe God is watching over us. Sorry if I was wallowing in self-pity there for a minute."

"You weren't," Dev protested, impressed with her inner strength and fortitude. He wasn't so sure he believed God was watching over her, though. Debra had believed in God, but that hadn't prevented her from dying too soon, taking their unborn child with them.

They ate in silence for a few minutes, before one of the nurses poked her head into the break room.

"Janelle? Sebastian's been assigned a room on the third floor. I've already called a report up to Shannon, the nurse who will be admitting him. We're pretty much ready to leave as soon as you are."

"I'm finished," Janelle said, jumping to her feet and quickly wrapping up what was left of her sandwich. "I'll eat the rest, later."

Devon rose to his feet, wishing there was more he could do for her. "Please call me if there's anything else you need," he murmured.

"Thanks Dev." She gave him a brief hug before turning to follow Phoebe towards Sebastian's room.

He watched her from the doorway, the faint citrus scent of her still clinging to his skin. He told himself that he should go home and get some rest. But for some reason, he couldn't seem to force his feet to move.

He stayed right where he was, watching as both Janelle and the gurney carrying Sebastian moved out of sight.

JANELLE DIDN'T GET much sleep that night, waking up every couple of hours when the nurse came into the room to check on Sebastian. His fever broke about six in the morning, which was a huge relief.

But she knew the little boy wasn't out of danger, yet. The fact of the matter was that he was four and a half years old and no matter how many times she told him to leave the catheter alone, she still found him picking at it, sometimes unconsciously.

Was Sebastian destined to have more infections then? If so, then maybe hemodialysis was a better option. She'd be willing to do whatever it took, even driving an hour one way to Madison three times per week.

"Nana, I'm hungry."

"Okay, let's order breakfast, shall we?" She was glad Sebastian was hungry. "What would you like? French toast sticks?"

"Yeah!" Sebastian nodded eagerly.

She placed a double order, so that she could share with him, and then decided she may as well give up on getting any more sleep. Besides, nothing else mattered as long as Sebastian was feeling better.

She was washing up in the bathroom when Sebastian's physician arrived. When she heard talking out in the room, she tossed down her hairbrush and quickly joined them.

"Hi, I'm Janelle, Sebastian's guardian," she introduced herself.

"Dr. Rawlings, nephrology specialist," he said giving her hand a shake. "I see you recently transferred Sebastian's care here."

She bit her lower lip and nodded. "I live here and work here, so I thought it was best to transfer his care. Why, is that a problem?"

"Not a problem, exactly, but you do realize if a kidney becomes available, you'll need to take him to Madison."

"Yes, I'm aware of that," Janelle said, meeting Dr. Rawlings serious gaze with one of her own. "However, I was led to believe it could take years before a kidney might become available."

"True, blood type B negative is a difficult match," Dr. Rawlings agreed. "And Sebastian isn't very high on the list at this point, since he's been tolerating peritoneal dialysis so well."

"I don't necessarily agree," Janelle said, trying not to display her frustration. "He's only four and keeping his catheter site clean is a challenge."

She thought Dr. Rawlings would argue, but he nodded his agreement. "I know, and I'm sure you're doing the best you can. But the fact is, his kidney failure just isn't bad enough right now to move him up the list."

She was glad Sebastian's kidney failure wasn't that bad, but the thought of waiting years for a transplant was just as daunting. She let out a heavy sigh. "I understand. What about hemodialysis? Is that an option?"

Dr. Rawlings hesitated, then shook his head. "I'm afraid not. Again, his creatinine, BUN, and electrolytes just aren't bad enough for that either. Truly his best option is to continue with peritoneal dialysis."

"All right," she murmured, determined to do whatever was best for Sebastian.

"Has the fluid been dwelling in his abdomen all night?" Dr. Rawlings asked.

"Yes. I was waiting for you to arrive before draining the fluid in case you wanted to see it."

"Great, then let's take a look, shall we?"

Janelle washed her hands and then manipulated the peritoneal dialysis catheter so that the fluid that was in Sebastian's abdominal cavity could drain out. This was the least invasive of the treatments available for kidney disease, and while it wasn't at all difficult, she still hadn't found anyone willing to do the task while she was at work.

"Looks good to me," Dr. Rawlings said, as the clear yellow fluid drained into the bag.

"Do you think we need to send it for culture?" Janelle asked.

"No need, probably won't grow anything with the antibiotics on board but I'd like him to get one more dose of IV antibiotics before you head home."

"Home?" Sebastian echoed, his attention momentarily deviating from the Disney channel when he heard the doctor's news. "We get to go home?"

Janelle's heart swelled at the excitement in Sebastian's eyes. She was so glad he was settling into his new life here in Crystal Lake. She sat down on the edge of his bed and gathered him into her arms. "Yes we do. Isn't that great news?"

He nodded and nestled against her. "After breakfast?" he asked.

"Maybe after lunch," Dr. Rawlings corrected as he logged into the computer to write his note.

"But that means I can't go to school," Sebastian protested, his lower lip trembling.

"Today is Saturday, there's no school on Saturdays remember?" Janelle reminded him. She was glad that Sebastian liked the four-year old kindergarten program she'd enrolled him in. The hours worked perfectly with his dialysis schedule, and so far the kids seemed to have accepted him, catheter and all.

"Can I play wif my friends?" he asked.

"We'll see," she promised, hoping that one of the little boys who lived close by might be able to come over for a few hours at least.

"Any other questions?" Dr. Rawlings asked as he logged off.

"No, I don't think so," Janelle said slowly. "He was so sick last night, I'm amazed at how well he's doing this morning. And I was afraid he'd need a new catheter."

"Kids are pretty resilient," Dr. Rawlings said. "They get sick fast, but then get better fast, too. Still, I'd keep a close eye on his temperature for the next few days, just in case. And make sure you give him all the oral antibiotics until they're gone."

"I will, thanks." When she was alone in the room with Sebastian, she tried to think of how she'd manage when she had to return to work next week. She'd used up every vacation day she had, and had dipped into her meager savings account too. Even if her boss did extend her leave of absence, how much longer could she go without a paycheck?

Not very long, that was for sure.

She closed her eyes and took several deep breaths, reaching out in prayer. God would show her the way. She just had to trust in Him and continue following His path.

When breakfast arrived a few minutes later, a sense of peace settled over her. Watching the way Sebastian dug into his meal with enthusiasm was enough to make her smile. Obviously Dr. Rawlings was right. Amazing how quickly Sebastian had returned to his old self.

The day shift nurse came in to check on Sebastian's abdominal dressing and to do a brief assessment. "Are you feeling better, Sebastian?"

He nodded, his eyes glued to the Disney movie on the television hanging on the wall.

"He's much better, thanks," Janelle said. "Dr. Rawlings mentioned being discharged after lunch."

"He gets his last dose of antibiotic around one o'clock, so as soon as that's infused you'll be able to take him home on oral medication."

"Sounds good," she agreed, even though she knew it wouldn't be easy to get Sebastian to take the oral medication in liquid form.

Shortly after the nurse left, there was another knock at the door.

"Come in," she called.

Her jaw dropped when she saw Devon enter the room, smiling sheepishly as he carried a huge box. "Hi," he greeted her awkwardly.

"Hi, what's in the box?" She rose to her feet and crossed over to greet him, surprised he'd come back to visit.

"This is a Play-Station that I had lying around, thought Sebastian here might be able to use it."

"Play-Station?" Once again, Sebastian's attention was pulled away from the television. "Can I see it?"

"Absolutely." Devon pulled the console out of the box and handed over the remote controls. Janelle didn't know much about how they worked, but clearly Sebastian knew all about them as he helped Devon put the pieces together.

"There, now you're all set," Devon declared with a grin.

"Aren't you gonna play with me?" Sebastian asked.

Devon glanced at her, with a questioning look in his eye.

"It's okay if you have things to do," she said, letting him off the hook. "I'm sure Sebastian can teach me how to play."

"I don't have to work until later this afternoon," Devon said in a low voice. "And I'm happy to play with Sebastian for a while if you have errands or something that you need to get done."

His generosity was touching. And even though he was giving her some free time, at the moment she couldn't even think of one thing that needed to be done. "Thanks Devon, I'm sure Sebastian would love to play with you for a while."

"Okay, Sebastian pick your game and I'll take you on."

"Goody!" Sebastian jumped up and down on the bed with enthusiasm. "Mario! I wanna play Mario!"

"You got it," Devon said picking up the game and inserting it into the console. He pulled up a chair next to Sebastian's bed and within minutes the two of them were in the throes of the video game.

Janelle ran her fingers through her hair, feeling self-conscious. Maybe she should take advantage of Devon being here with Sebastian. She could run home, take a shower and change out of her wrinkled clothes.

It took her a minute to realize that she secretly wanted to look nice for Devon. Which was ridiculous. He was here out of friendship, after all, she knew only too well that men weren't interested in a woman who happened to be the legal guardian to a young boy with special medical needs.

So instead of running home, she stayed where she was, curled up on the sleeper sofa that doubled as a twin bed for parents staying overnight. She dozed off for a while, startling awake when the nurse came into the room, interrupting the marathon game.

"Time for Sebastian's peritoneal dialysis exchange," Andrea announced.

Janelle rubbed the sleep from her eyes. "I can do it," she said stretching out her cramped legs.

"No!" Sebastian shouted, his gaze glued to the game. "Don't wanna do my exchange. Me and Dev are playing a game."

"We can pause the game, Sebastian," Devon explained in a low patient voice. "We'll start right back up where we left off."

"Don't wanna," Sebastian repeated stubbornly.

Janelle stepped forward, putting a reassuring hand on Sebastian's back. "Come on, Sebastian, you know doing the exchange only takes a few minutes."

Devon hit the pause button, despite Sebastian's protest. "You need to listen to your Aunt Janelle, Sebastian."

Ironically, the authoritative tone in Devon's voice worked. "Okay," Sebastian repeated reluctantly.

"Game time is just about over anyway," Janelle said as she set out the supplies she'd need. "We need to eat lunch and then once you get your last dose of antibiotic we can go home."

"Hey, that's great news," Devon said. "That means no surgery, right?"

"Right." She concentrated on making sure she didn't contaminate the catheter tip as she connected the new peritoneal dialysis solution so that it could slowly infuse into Sebastian's abdomen. A process that didn't hurt him at all, so normally he never seemed to mind.

Janelle was keenly aware of Devon's gaze watching her. She'd done this exchange three times a day for the past three weeks, but her fingers suddenly felt awkward and clumsy.

"So the fluid stays in his abdomen for the next few hours?" Devon asked, the expression on his face showing genuine interest.

"That's right," she said with a smile. "Then we drain out the old fluid and infuse a new bag that dwells overnight. Since Sebastian's kidneys don't work as well as they should, this helps draw toxins out of his blood stream."

"Amazing," Devon murmured.

She finished her task and then cleaned up the supplies

and washed her hands. "What would you like for lunch, Sebastian?"

"Chicken fingers," the boy said automatically picking his favorite.

"Why did I bother asking?" Janelle asked with a sigh. She glanced at Devon. "We're allowed to order parent trays, I'm happy to share one with you."

"No thanks, I ate a huge breakfast before I came and I like to eat just prior to the start of my shift. But please, eat something. You didn't get much last night."

The memory of the simple meal they'd shared in the break room of the ER flashed in her mind. The sudden intimacy that sprang between them had lingered in her mind, long after he was gone.

She ordered a salad, and when their food arrived, Devon still didn't show any sign that he intended to leave. Not that she wanted him to, but still, she felt bad taking up all his free time.

When the nurse came in to hang Sebastian's antibiotic, she glanced at her watch. "Good news, Sebastian. We'll be able to head home in less than an hour."

"Great, we'll have time to play one more game," Devon said, settling back in his seat.

"You don't need to stay, I'm sure you have other things to do."

Devon shrugged. "I'll follow you home that way I can connect the game console to your television for you."

"Oh, no, I couldn't possibly accept such an expensive gift," she protested.

Devon raised a brow. "It's not a gift, I'm letting you and Sebastian borrow it for a while. My nephews are older now and it's not doing any good sitting at the bottom of my closet."

How could she refuse to allow Sebastian to *borrow* the game? Very simply, she couldn't. "Thank you," she murmured.

The hour flew by and soon they were packing up to leave. Janelle tucked the bottle of oral antibiotic solution in her purse, as Devon packed the game back into its box.

She felt bad taking Devon out of his way, but since she had no clue how to set up the game, there wasn't much she could do about it. "I live in the Crain's townhouse just off Main Street," she told him, as they walked out into the bright April sunshine. The air was a little cool, but she was thrilled that spring was on the way. "I rent one side, but the other side is empty at the moment. The doctor who was living in the other side just bought a house."

"I know exactly where the townhouse is," Devon said. "I'll meet you there."

She was blessed to have such good friends in Julie and Derek for letting her rent the townhouse, and in Devon who had gone out of his way to support her with Sebastian. For the first time since Sebastian's fever had risen out of control, she felt optimistic about the future.

This was what she loved most about living in Crystal Lake. The sense of community; everyone helping each other as needed.

It took a few minutes for Janelle to get Sebastian secured in his car seat, so when she headed home, she wasn't too surprised to see that Devon had beat her to the townhouse.

When she pulled up the driveway, Devon approached her vehicle, a frown deeply furrowed in his brow. "Janelle, I need you to stay inside the car, okay?"

"What? Why?" She craned her neck in an attempt to see around him.

"Someone broke into your house," Devon said in a grim tone.

"What? Are you sure?"

"Yes, I am. Sorry, Janelle, but it looks like you've been the victim of a robbery."

3

"A robbery? Someone broke in? Why?" Janelle's horrified facial expression tore at his heart. After everything she and the boy had been through, this was the last thing she needed.

Devon flashed a reassuring smile. "I don't know, but please stay here, okay?" He glanced at Sebastian who was looking a little sleepy. "I don't think anyone is still hanging around, but it would be best to make sure."

"Alright," Janelle agreed, her expression troubled.

He stepped back from the car, shaking his head and wondering why bad things always seemed to happen to good people. He turned and walked back up to the front porch.

Devon carefully examined the smashed door frame, taking care not to touch anything. It looked as if the door knob had been smashed with a blunt object, like a baseball bat or a hammer.

Or the heel of someone's boot. To be honest, the door-jamb wasn't the sturdiest he'd ever seen. There wasn't a lot of crime in Crystal Lake so nobody really paid for high level security systems.

Although it would have been nice if Janelle had used the dead bolt.

Still, he knew that if someone really wanted to get inside, they'd find a way. Either through the patio doors overlooking Crystal Lake or through a window. Kids? Maybe. He'd know more when he was able to investigate what was taken.

Either way, being robbed was hardly Janelle's fault.

He scowled and raked a hand through his hair. There hadn't been any reports of robberies discussed in their roll call yesterday, but he imagined there would soon be others. These types of home invasions tended to happen in clusters, especially if teenagers were involved.

Thankfully, Janelle and Sebastian hadn't been home. Just the thought of what might have happened if they had been brought a flash of anger.

The wail of sirens echoed through the air, indicating reinforcements were on the way. Good thing, because he was having a hard time playing the civilian role.

He wished he had his weapon, but he'd left it at home. He knew the hospital wouldn't allow him to carry it inside since he wasn't officially on duty. Besides, carrying a gun around a four-year old wasn't smart.

When Deputy Zack Crain pulled in behind Janelle, Dev walked down to meet him. Zack was Julie Crain's brother and the two of them owned the side-by-side townhouses, even though neither one of them lived there any longer. Zack and Merry had gotten married about eighteen months ago and now lived on the other side of the lake.

"What happened?" Zack asked with obvious concern.

"I don't honestly know. Janelle spent the night at the hospital with Sebastian, so she wasn't here. I was planning to meet her here, and arrived first. That's when I found the front door smashed in."

"Sebastian? Is he okay?" Zack asked, crossing over to peer into Janelle's back seat. He waved at the little boy who glanced up at him with a tired smile.

Dev couldn't help wondering if the child was tired from the peritoneal dialysis treatments or if this was just a normal part of having kidney failure? "He's fine, although you should probably get all the details from Janelle."

As if on cue, Janelle slid out from the driver's seat. "Hi Zack. Can I go inside to see what, if anything, was taken?"

"Not yet, but soon," Zack promised. "Just give us some time to make sure it's safe, okay?"

"Why would anyone pick my place to rob?" she asked, rubbing her hands over her arms as if chilled. "I don't have anything worth stealing."

"I'm sure it's nothing personal," Zack assured her.

"Have there been other reported robberies?" Dev asked.

Zack hesitated and shook his head. "Not that I'm aware of. But maybe others haven't been noticed yet either."

Dev nodded, and couldn't help thinking the timing of the robbery was significant. Janelle and Sebastian had been gone for roughly sixteen hours, and it was likely that the break-in had happened sometime during the night or the early morning.

Or was it possible the crook had watched her leave the house with Sebastian and then took advantage of the fact they were gone to rob the place?

He scowled, not liking that scenario.

"Let's go," Zack said, clapping Dev on the shoulder.

Dev followed his colleague into the house, sucking in a harsh breath when he immediately noticed the empty spot where the television had probably been.

Zack whistled under his breath. "I hope Janelle has good insurance."

Yeah, somehow Dev wasn't so sure she did, but he didn't say anything as they continued sweeping through the townhouse. It didn't take long to verify the place was empty.

"I'll get Janelle," Dev offered, heading back outside. The moment he stepped out on the porch, Janelle stepped forward, holding Sebastian in her arms.

"I'm sorry, but your television has been stolen," Dev said, wanting to warn her. "The good news is that the robbers didn't trash the place."

Janelle nodded, although she went pale when she saw the missing television. "It wasn't even an expensive one," she said in a low voice.

"Anything else missing?" Dev asked.

She nodded slowly, tears welling in her eyes. "My notebook computer. And my router."

Devon hated seeing her so upset. "You might want to check your room, in case any jewelry is missing."

She sucked in a quick breath and rushed into her bedroom. Dev watched from the doorway, battling a wave of helplessness.

"Lisa's ring is gone," Janelle whispered, lifting tortured eyes to his. "The only thing I had that belonged to my sister. I was saving it for Sebastian."

Dev didn't know what to say to make things better. He crossed over and put a reassuring arm around her shoulders, grateful when she leaned against him.

He silently vowed that he'd do whatever was necessary in order to find the jerk who did this.

· · ·

JANELLE LEANED AGAINST DEVON, mentally as well as physically exhausted. She couldn't believe Lisa's ring was gone. It wasn't super expensive, but it was gold and had a ruby stone, the birthstone shared by both Lisa and Sebastian.

"Nana? Can me and Dev play Mario again?" Sebastian asked in a plaintive tone.

She swallowed hard and straightened up, knowing she couldn't afford to lean on anyone, no matter how nice Devon had been over the past twenty-four hours. "I'm sorry, but we don't have a television. It's broken," she added hastily, unwilling to give Sebastian a reason to be afraid.

His tiny brow puckered in a frown. "Who breaked it?"

"Hey, how about I bring my television over for a while?" Devon offered. "I can't use it while I'm at work anyway."

Janelle began to shake her head, but Sebastian's face lit up with excitement. "Goody," he cowed, bobbling up and down in her arms to the point she had to bend over and set him on the ground. "Go get it, Dev. Go get it!"

She wanted to protest but sensed that would be a fruitless endeavor. "Thank you, Devon," she said in a soft tone. "I'm not sure why you're being so nice to us, but I want you to know how much I appreciate it."

Dev shrugged, the tips of his ears turning red with embarrassment. "It's really not a problem, but I don't like leaving you here alone with a broken front door."

"I've already called Frank from the hardware store," Zack said entering the room. "He's on his way to fix it, until I can get a new door in." He glanced at her and took out a small notebook. "I'll need a list of everything that's missing."

"I'll be back in a few minutes," Devon promised, leaving

the room. Janelle had to fight back the urge to beg him to stay.

Ridiculous, really, for one thing Zack was also a cop and a great guy. For another, he happened to be her landlord. She gave herself a mental shake, chalking up her wacky emotions to a night without much sleep.

The list of missing items was pathetically short, and when Zack asked the name of her insurance company, she was forced to admit she didn't have renter's insurance.

Zack groaned. "I don't think my insurance is going to cover your things," he informed her.

"I understand," she hastened to assure him. "It's my fault, Zack, I certainly know better. It's just that I've been more focused on my sister and Sebastian..." her voice trailed off on the pathetic excuse.

The truth of the matter was that even though renter's insurance wasn't expensive, she hadn't been able to afford it. Not when she wasn't working nearly as many hours as she used to.

Zack sighed and turned away. "Okay, I have someone coming to dust for finger prints on the area around the door, where the television was, your computer and the jewelry box."

"Sounds good." Janelle forced a smile. "Thanks again for coming so quickly."

"It's no problem, after all, I don't like the thought of anyone breaking into my townhouse any more than you do," Zack admitted. "Crystal Lake is normally a safe place to live."

Janelle nodded in agreement, because the small town family atmosphere was one of the main reasons she loved living here. "Well, I'm sure you'll find out who did this."

"How is Sebastian?" Zack asked as they walked back into the main living area.

"He's fine, had a little infection but is already doing much better." She eyed the clock, making a mental note to give her nephew his antibiotic at dinnertime.

Zack's phone rang and he stepped away to answer it. Janelle could tell he was talking to his wife, Merry, and she couldn't help the ping of envy at the love that shone brightly between the two of them.

An old rusty blue pick-up truck pulled to a stop in front of her house and she smiled when she saw Frank Gebheart get out from behind the wheel, his tool belt cinched tightly beneath his round belly.

Zack finished his call and strode out to meet with Frank, making it clear what he needed done. Soon her small town-house was full of people, techs dusting for fingerprints, Frank hammering on the door, and Devon setting up his wide screen television along with the video console in the space where her smaller TV once sat.

The entire process didn't take long. The crime scene techs and Frank left first, followed by Zack. Devon had returned already dressed in his uniform so he could head directly to work.

"Thanks again," Janelle murmured as he handed Sebastian the hand-held controller.

"Not a problem," he assured her with a smile. Their eyes locked and just like the night before, she found herself mesmerized by the intensity of his gaze.

She forced herself to look away, afraid he'd notice the longing in her eyes. "Well, at least I know the robbers won't be back since they've already taken everything of value."

Devon scowled as he headed for the door. "Trust me, I'll

be driving by frequently throughout my shift to make sure they don't."

"Thanks." She stood by the door, watching as Devon strode confidently toward his cruiser. The way he tipped his hat to her before sliding in behind the wheel made her blush with awareness.

Watching him drive away, she felt more alone than ever.

DEV HATED LEAVING Janelle and Sebastian in the townhouse, even though logically he knew they'd be perfectly fine after the repairs Frank had done to the front door.

Roll call didn't take long and he was disturbed to hear that Janelle's place was the only reported break-in. They were lucky to get some fingerprints, but it would take a while to get them processed through the database.

The only other item of interest was a small bag of crystal meth that was found in the bathroom of the school. Dev couldn't deny the fact that the two incidents could very well be related. Drug addicts were known to steal anything in sight in order to support their habit.

He hated the thought of drugs being brought into their small town. Of course, drugs were just about everywhere, so he couldn't say he was completely surprised.

Once roll call was over, he headed outside to his vehicle and made his usual sweep of the lake. They didn't have a huge influx of tourists yet, that would come in the summer months. Although they used to get hikers, but they'd dwindled off since the big fire along the hiking trail last fall.

Dev was glad to see that there were signs of spring. Some slender seedlings were sprouting amidst the blackened soil. It would take several years for the trees to grow back, but at least the process had started. And the woods overshadowing the north side of the lake were miraculously untouched.

As he drove around the area, he couldn't help thinking about what Janelle and Sebastian were up to. He liked the idea that the two of them were sitting and playing his game on the television he'd loaned them.

If anyone deserved a break, they did.

The hours seemed to drag by more slowly than usual, and when it was time for dinner, he had to force himself not to drive straight to Janelle's townhouse.

Instead, he pulled over to park on Main Street and headed into Rosie's diner. Josie, the owner and waitress hailed him from the doorway.

"Hey, Dev, should I get you a plate of the usual?"

Since his usual was the special pot roast, potatoes, and carrots, he nodded. "Absolutely, thanks."

Josie placed his order then came over with a pitcher of water, filling his glass for him. "I heard about the break-in at the Crain place. Do you have any suspects yet?"

He shouldn't have been caught off guard at her blunt question. Josie was the town gossip, and he often wished the police network was as good as the town grapevine.

"Not yet, but we'll figure out who's responsible, don't worry." He purposefully infused confidence into his tone. The last thing they needed was for the town folk to go into panic mode.

"Such a shame," Josie went on. She set down the pitcher and propped her hand on her hip. "To think that someone would take a television away from a young child and a sickly one at that! What is this world coming to?"

He didn't have a good answer and honestly, Josie didn't need one.

"Well, I sure hope you find that no-good son-of-a-gun as soon as possible."

"That's the plan."

Josie glared at him for a moment, then grabbed the pitcher of water and swept away. But before he could relax, she came back, this time carrying a large plastic container.

"Dev, I need you to take this over to Janelle and Sebastian for me."

He eyed it warily. "What's inside?"

She rolled her eyes. "Fried toad-skins." When he blinked in shock, she roared with laughter. "Tonight's special, on the house. Will you take the time to run it over to her?"

How could he say no? "Of course, Josie. It's nice of you to think about them."

"They're one of us, and we take care of our own." With that, Josie disappeared back behind the counter.

Devon couldn't deny that he'd miss this place if he ever did get a response from one of his applications,but carrying food to a young mother in need and trying to find kids who were breaking into empty homes to steal or doing drugs wasn't exactly what he had envisioned for the rest of his life, either.

He wanted to fight real crime, to make a difference. The same way his older brother Steve had.

By the time he finished his meal, dusk was falling over the horizon. He carried the heavy container of Josie's special outside, and decided it would be easier to walk the couple of blocks to Janelle's townhouse than to drive over.

As he approached her townhouse, he noticed a dark silver sedan parked on the other side of the road. He frowned, trying to see if the car was empty, when abruptly the headlights flashed on, momentarily blinding him.

He shielded his face, and tried to catch the license plate

number, but was a second too late. The car backed up, turned around and quickly disappeared around a curve.

A chill snaked down his back. Was he imagining things? The actions of the driver seemed suspicious. Had he parked there in order to watch Janelle's house?

And if so, why?

4

Janelle was thrilled to see that Sebastian seemed to be doing so well, he'd been so enthralled in his game that he hadn't even asked for a friend to come over.

She'd finished cleaning up the mess the crime scene techs had left behind and now stood in the kitchen, trying to think of something to make for dinner. Her fridge was pretty empty, she'd need to grocery shop in the morning. A loud knock at her front door startled her from her thoughts, and she took a moment to put a hand over her racing heart, before crossing over to peer through the window to see who was out there.

"Devon?" she asked as she opened the door. She tried to squash a wave of pleasure at seeing him again. "What are you doing here?"

He lifted a container. "Josie sent you a healthy serving of her Saturday night special."

"Pot roast?" she asked with a smile, opening the door and gesturing for him to come in.

"Yep."

"Dev!" Sebastian abandoned his game to come rushing over to greet his new hero. "Did you come to play wif me?"

"I'm sorry, Sebastian, but I'm working tonight," Devon said. "Are you hungry? I brought dinner."

"Will you stay to eat with us?" Sebastian asked.

"Sweetie, Devon already told you he's working," Janelle quickly interjected. "But if you eat all your dinner and take your medicine, I'll play another game with you before bedtime."

"Okay," Sebastian agreed, although she could tell the little boy was still disappointed that Devon wasn't going to stick around.

"Janelle, do you know anyone who drives a silver sedan?" Dev asked as she carried Josie's container of food into the kitchen.

She glanced at him in surprise. "No, why?"

He shrugged and shook his head. "No reason, I don't want to alarm you."

She stared at him. "I'm already scared, Devon so just spit it out already. Why are you asking about a silver car?"

He winced. "I'm probably making a big deal out of nothing," he warned. "But I noticed a silver car parked across the street from the townhouse. Could be someone staying at the Crystal Lake Motel, though."

She shivered and tried not to let her imagination run wild. "The motel has a parking lot, why would they choose to park along the road?"

"Listen, just ignore me," Devon said, rubbing the back of his neck, looking embarrassed. "I'm sure it's nothing. I promised you I'd drive by frequently and I will continue to do that. No need to worry."

Janelle wished it was easy to shut down the worry gene, but unfortunately it seemed that she'd only gotten worse in the weeks since she'd taken custody of Sebastian, rather than better. "I'll try," she said, trying to hide the doubt in her tone.

"I'm sorry, Janelle," Devon said with a grimace. "I shouldn't have mentioned it."

She lifted her troubled gaze to his. "There's no reason for the robbers to come back here, right? This wasn't a personal attack against us."

"Absolutely not," Dev assured her. He crossed over and put his arms around her in a quick hug. It disturbed her how much she longed to lean against him, absorbing his strength. "Don't think about it, okay? I promise to watch over your place."

It was on the tip of her tongue to point out that he wouldn't be on duty twenty-four seven, but she forced a smile and stepped back. "I appreciate your support, Dev."

"I only wish I could do more," he said in a serious tone. "Call me if you need anything."

"I will," she agreed although she knew that Devon had certainly done enough for her and for Sebastian. She walked him to the door, sneaking a glance up and down the street to make sure there weren't any strange cars lingering.

Which of course there weren't.

"Where's your car?" she asked with a frown.

"I walked over from the café," he said. "I'll see you later," he said as he walked back out toward the road.

She lifted her hand in a nonchalant wave as Devon glanced back at her, then closed the door, locked it and shot the dead-bolt home.

The rest of her evening flew by, and soon she finished infusing his last bag of peritoneal dialysis. She quickly cleaned up the supplies and then crossed over to tuck Sebastian into bed.

"Are you ready to say your bedtime prayers?" she asked, sitting on the edge of his bed.

He nodded, pressing his tiny palms together and squeezing his eyes shut. "God bless Nana, Devon, and my angel Mommy," Sebastian said sleepily. "Amen."

"Amen," she echoed, blinking the moisture from her eyes. She leaned down to press a kiss on Sebastian's forehead and when his arms wrapped tightly around her neck, she pressed him close, savoring the embrace.

"I love you, Sebastian," she whispered in his ear.

"I wuv you, too, Nana."

In that moment all her fears about her finances, her job, even being the victim of a robbery, flew right out the window. Nothing was more important than this little boy. Sebastian was a precious gift she'd cherish forever.

"Goodnight," she said when he finally drew away.

"G'night," he answered, turning over and throwing his arm around his stuffed angel.

Janelle made sure the nightlight was glowing in the corner of his room before she left, leaving the door ajar the way he preferred.

A wave of exhaustion hit hard, reminding her that it had been a long day and that she hadn't had much sleep the night before. Even though it was early, she moved through the townhouse, shutting off the lights and double checking the locks on her doors, before getting ready for bed.

As she walked past the living room window, a pair of headlights coming down the street made her stop abruptly, her heart leaping in fear. But then they passed by without stopping.

Idiot, she admonished herself. There was no reason to be afraid.

Devon would protect her.

. . .

CONSIDERING IT WAS SATURDAY NIGHT, Devon was glad things weren't too busy. He'd been called to a fight at Pete's Pub, but by the time he'd arrived, the two men had been separated by the townsfolk, leaving him with nothing more to do than to take care of the paperwork. He didn't hesitate to issue assault and battery charges and disorderly conduct charges to both men, one sporting a black eye, the other a fat lip.

Apparently they'd been fighting over a woman, who'd wasted no time in high-tailing it out of the place once the fight broke out. Not that he blamed her.

Devon dutifully filled out the paperwork, and then made sure both men were sober enough to drive themselves home. He also jotted down their license plate numbers along with the make and model of their vehicles, just in case.

Not that he suspected either one of them of being the perp who'd performed the robbery. Still, it didn't hurt to be cautious.

He felt terrible for scaring Janelle, earlier. He'd driven by her townhouse several times and hadn't seen anything the least bit suspicious. He shouldn't have mentioned the stupid car, especially when he hadn't gotten a good look at it anyway.

As the end of his shift approached, Devon took one more leisurely drive down Main Street, making sure things were quiet and peaceful before heading to the Sheriff's department headquarters.

He headed home and changed his clothes, but wasn't the least bit tired. Moving restlessly around his house, he found he couldn't settle down.

Logically he knew Janelle and Sebastian weren't in danger. He'd imagined the driver of the silver car was staking out her townhouse. And there really wasn't any reason for the robber to return.

So why couldn't he relax?

Dev forced himself to climb into bed, where he tossed and turned for the next hour. Finally he gave up. He threw on a comfy sweatshirt and jeans before heading back outside to his personal vehicle.

He drove back to Janelle's townhouse, reassured that all was quiet. The windows were mostly dark, although there was a dim light coming from Sebastian's room.

He pulled in front of her house and shut off the engine. The spring air was a bit cool, but not enough to bother him. He ratcheted back his seat and stretched out, making sure he could see her front door.

Dev let out a pent up sigh, feeling calmer now that he was close at hand, on the off-chance that Janelle would need him. He told himself he wouldn't stay too long, just long enough to unwind after his shift.

The stars twinkled overhead and he couldn't help remembering the way Debra had believed God was watching over them from the heavens.

It had taken him a long time to realize the pain of losing her and their unborn child wouldn't ever go away completely. Granted he didn't think about them every day, not any more.

But there were times like this, when he felt alone in the world that the bitter-sweet memories would return.

He tore his gaze from the velvet-black sky and looked over at Janelle's townhouse.

Letting go of the past wasn't easy, but he knew he needed

to keep focused on the present and on dedicating his life to making a difference in the world.

JANELLE WOKE UP EARLY, feeling refreshed after having a decent night's sleep.

She couldn't hear any sound from Sebastian's room and quickly freshened up in the bathroom, enjoying a few moments of privacy. Not that she resented caring for her nephew, but becoming a full time mother had been a bit of an adjustment.

Okay, make that a massive adjustment.

She ran a brush through her hair and then headed into the kitchen to start a pot of coffee. Sebastian would be up soon, the kid had an amazing internal alarm clock, and she began to make a mental list of things she needed to get done.

Making breakfast and attending church were her priorities, followed by grocery shopping if they wanted anything to eat for the rest of the week. But then she really needed to figure out a daycare situation of some sort in order to return to work on Monday morning.

She headed into the living room to tidy up the controllers from Devon's play-station, in case he wanted to come and pick it up in the near future. Glancing out the front window had become a nervous habit and when she noticed a black truck sitting directly in front of her house, she stifled a scream.

The robbers were back!

She rushed to the front closet and pulled out a baseball bat. She yanked open the front door and rushed outside, prepared to scream loud enough for the entire Crystal Lake population to hear her.

"Leave us alone!" she shouted brandishing the baseball bat like a sword. "The police are on the way!"

To her horror the driver's side door popped open and a dark haired man climbed out. "Janelle, calm down. It's me, Devon!"

"Dev?" She stood there for a moment, as the fear drained away leaving her feeling weak and foolish. Then she got mad. "What are you doing here? You scared me to death!"

"I'm sorry," he said holding his hands up as if to reassure her he wasn't armed. "Did you really call the sheriff's department? If so, we'd better let them know it's a false alarm."

She slowly lowered the bat, letting out her breath in a sigh. "No, I didn't call them. I reacted without thinking."

He opened his mouth as if to chastise her, but then closed it again. He scrubbed his hands over his face and for the first time she realized he must have been there all night.

"Why in the world did you sleep in your car?" she asked, truly bewildered. Hadn't he told her she wasn't in danger? Or had something happened late last night?

"I didn't mean to fall asleep," he admitted with a self-depreciating smile. "I only intended to be here for a couple of hours."

"So you didn't see anything suspicious?" she pressed, needing to know the truth. Heaven knew, she'd already planned to be on the alert for any sign of a silver car following her.

"Nothing," he said with confidence. "And really, I'm sorry I scared you."

"Well, since I scared you, too, I think we're even." She gestured toward the townhouse. "I have coffee if you'd like a cup before heading out."

His face broke into a relieved grin. "I would love some coffee. Cars are not meant for sleeping, that's for sure."

She laughed and shook her head. "I still can't believe you did that."

"Me either." He came up beside her and gently pried the bat from her clenched fingers. "You really should have called the police first," he murmured.

She sighed. "Yeah, I know."

Their arms brushed as they headed inside and she tried to tell herself that the tingling sensation was nothing more than her overactive imagination. She headed into the kitchen and pulled two coffee mugs out of the cupboard.

"Cream or sugar?" she asked, glancing at him over her shoulder. Her breath caught in her throat at how handsome he looked standing there with his shadowed jaw and sleep tousled hair.

Whoa, what was wrong with her? She needed to stop thinking of Devon as a man she was interested in. He was simply a good friend, nothing more.

"Black is fine," he said, his gaze lingering on hers. Was it her imagination or was there a flicker of awareness in his eyes?

"Dev!" Sebastian said in excitement as he padded into the room, clutching his stuffed angel like a lifeline. "You came back!"

She tried to hide a wince, certain that it hadn't been Devon's intention to be sucked back into another game with Sebastian.

"Sure did," Dev said with a broad smile. "But I think you have a few things to take care of first, don't you?"

"No I don't," Sebastian said defiantly.

"I'm pretty sure you need to drain your peritoneal dialysis first and then eat breakfast, right Janelle?"

She was amazed he remembered. "That's right. I need you to lie down on the sofa for a little while to drain while I make breakfast."

Sebastian's lower lip trembled. "I don't wanna."

Her heart ached for the little boy, but at the same time, she knew she needed to be firm, for his own good.

"Come on, champ, I'll sit next to you for a while," Dev offered.

"Really?" Sebastian's blue eyes instantly brightened. "Why can't we play a game while I'm draining?"

Dev glanced at her curiously and she lifted her hands up in a helpless gesture. "No reason, I guess. Does this mean you want to stay for breakfast?" she asked.

"I don't want to put you out," he hedged. But she had to smile when the rumbling in his stomach gave him away.

"Can we have French toast?" Sebastian asked as he climbed onto the sofa and obligingly stretched out giving plenty of room for her to access his catheter.

"Sure," she agreed. She pulled out the necessary supplies and then returned to the kitchen to wash her hands. She was keenly aware of Devon watching her every move. He gave the impression that he was truly interested, not simply gawking as she opened the clamp to allow the fluid in his abdomen to drain.

"I'm amazed that something so simple can be lifesaving to a child," Dev said in a low voice.

"It really is incredible," she agreed. "And it's not that difficult to do the exchanges. Unfortunately, the concept still scares people off."

He frowned. "So who watches him while you're at work?"

She bit her lower lip and shrugged. "No one yet," she said, avoiding the full story of how she was out of paid time off allowed under the family/medical leave act. She didn't want to dump her problems on Devon, so she quickly turned and headed into the kitchen to start breakfast.

She enjoyed listening as Dev and Seb played video game as she cooked. This was what how she imagined her life would be like with Lane. Only he hadn't wanted anything to do with her young nephew.

His loss, but she couldn't deny his rude departure still rankled. Being angry at him was useless, but she was upset with herself for wasting the last year of her life dating him. Lane hadn't been worth five minutes of her time, but obviously she'd been blind to his faults.

When she finished with the French toast, she washed her hands once again and went back over to disconnect Sebastian's drainage bag. She expected Dev to be disgusted by the yellow fluid filling the bag, but as before he intently watched everything she was doing.

"Just give me a few minutes, and we can eat breakfast," she said, carrying the bag toward the bathroom.

When she emerged a few minutes later, she was surprised to see that both Devon and Sebastian were in the kitchen waiting for her. She'd already washed up, so she pulled out her chair and sat down.

"I'm hungry," Sebastian said, eyeing up the stack of French toast.

"We need to pray first," she reminded him. Devon looked surprised, but he took his cue from Sebastian, clasping his hands together and bowing his head. "Dear Lord, we thank You for this wonderful food we are about to eat. We ask that You watch over us and guide us on Your chosen path as we begin our day, Amen."

"Amen," Sebastian and Dev said simultaneously.

She smiled, pleased at their response.

"When are you scheduled to go back to work?" Dev asked, as he held the plate of French toast out for her.

"Tomorrow morning. But I'm sure I can get one of the nurses I work with to cover my shift if I can't find someone to watch Sebastian."

"I'll do it," Devon offered.

Her mouth dropped open in shock and she wondered if she'd really heard him correctly. "Do what?"

"I'll watch Sebastian tomorrow. I have Monday and Tuesday off work, so it's no problem."

She was stunned speechless by his generous offer. As much as she didn't want to take advantage of Devon's friend-ship, she also knew that she needed to get back to work in order to pay her next month's rent.

"I don't know what to say," she finally managed. "Are you serious?"

"Absolutely. I've been watching you and it doesn't look that difficult to do his exchanges. Of course, I'll need to practice, but I'm sure I can manage."

Janelle stared at him for several seconds. Was Dev's offer an answer to her prayers? Or a complication she couldn't afford?

She was afraid she'd end up depending on him, far more than she should.

5

Devon watched the play of emotions across Janelle's face, wondering if he'd overstepped his bounds.

Why had he offered to babysit anyway? Just looking at Sebastian made his heart ache for what he'd lost. Before he could try to backpedal, she slowly nodded.

"All right, then. Thank you, Devon."

"You're welcome." He stared down at his plate of French toast for a moment before picking up his fork. Two days wasn't the end of the world. He just needed to help her out until she found someone to watch Sebastian on a regular basis.

"Yay! I get to play with Dev!" Sebastian shouted.

"That's right, but now it's time to eat breakfast, okay?" Janelle said. "And then we have to get ready to go to church."

Dev shouldn't have been surprised by the announcement, after all, most of the town went to church on Sunday. He swallowed hard, wondering if she expected him to come along.

He hadn't been inside the church since Debra's funeral.

"Dev?"

He jerked his head up, realizing Janelle had been talking to him. "I'm sorry, what did you say?"

She tipped her head to the side, regarding him thoughtfully. "I asked if you were working again today."

"Yeah, I'm on duty tonight, starting at three in the afternoon. That's the main reason I have the next two days off."

"I work the early shift on Monday and Tuesday, seven to three-thirty, so you'll still have some time to relax." She paused, then continued, "I owe you, big, Devon. I'm out of paid leave and really need to work to avoid going into debt."

The puckered frown in her brow made him glad he'd impulsively offered to help. "It's no problem, Janelle. You don't owe me anything, you saved my life two years ago, remember?"

"The doctors saved your life," she corrected with a smile. "I just helped."

He clearly remembered the way she'd held onto his hand in the ER, talking to him and reassuring him that everything would be okay. Yeah, the doctor's skills had helped, but emotionally, he'd clung to Janelle's voice like a lifeline.

"Are you going to come to church wif us?" Sebastian asked around a mouthful of food.

"Chew and swallow first, then talk," Janelle told him.

Dev felt trapped by Sebastian's wide blue eyes. He hadn't intended to attend church services, but then again, he needed to learn how to do the peritoneal dialysis exchanges too. It would look pretty obvious if he left before church and then came back afterwards.

"I'm sure Devon has things he needs to get done before work," Janelle said, giving him an out. The intensity of her gaze, as if she knew exactly why he didn't want to attend, made him feel vulnerable.

Janelle had been here in Crystal Lake long enough to know he'd lost his fiancée. But she'd never asked him about his loss.

And no one knew that Debra had been pregnant. He'd never told anyone about that fact.

"I, uh, don't know," he hedged. What was wrong with him? Why hadn't he taken the excuse Janelle had offered?

"Finish your breakfast, Sebastian. We have to infuse another bag through your catheter before we go."

"Okay," Sebastian agreed, popping another large bite of French toast in his mouth, smearing maple syrup across his chin.

Dev was impressed at how well the boy accepted the treatments he needed to have—what had Janelle said—three times a day.

"More coffee?" Janelle offered, rising to her feet and walking toward the pot.

"Yes, please." Sitting at the kitchen table, sharing a meal with Janelle and Sebastian gave him a pang in the region of his heart. This was what he should have had with Debra and his own son or daughter.

No point in looking backward besides, this cozy family scene wasn't what he wanted anymore. He needed to make a difference in the world. He wanted to fight crime and to help keep cities safe for other kids.

The same way his brother had.

When breakfast was finished, he stood and then carried his dirty dishes over to the sink. He hid a smile when Sebastian copied his actions, even though the little boy couldn't even reach the counter.

"Thanks Sebastian," Janelle said, taking the plate from

him. She took a clean dishcloth and efficiently wiped down the child's sticky hands and face. "Time for your medicine."

Sebastian scrunched his face into an expression of distaste. "Do I hav'ta?"

"Yes," Devon spoke up firmly. "No games until you take your medicine."

Sebastian gamely swallowed the thick liquid, wrinkling his nose at the taste before dashing into the living room.

"I'd like to watch the exchange," Dev said.

"Watch?" She echoed, lifting a sardonic brow. "You need to actually practice doing the exchange."

He knew she was right. "Okay, but you're going to walk me through it, right?"

"Of course." She rinsed the dishes and set them in the dishwasher. "Wash your hands and I'll show you how to set up the supplies."

She talked him through the entire process and his fingers felt large and clumsy as he disconnected the catheter and hung a new bag.

"The biggest threat is infection," she said quietly. "That's why you have to be careful not to contaminate anything."

Remembering how sick Sebastian had been made him realize just how high risk this process really was. Oh, it didn't look complicated, but one wrong move could cause a life threatening infection. He held his breath as he worked, feeling a bead of sweat trickling down the side of his face. He didn't breathe normally until he was finished.

"Good job," Janelle said. "Now open the clamp on the tubing, just part way because if the fluid runs in too fast it will cause stomach cramps."

He carefully adjusted the flow and then stepped back, curling his fingers into fists to stop his fingers from shaking.

He felt as if he'd run five miles. He wiped the sweat from his brow with the edge of his sweatshirt.

"How long will it take to run the fluid in?" he asked.

"Sebastian tolerates about an hour." She gathered up the empty wrappers and carried everything over into the kitchen.

"Can we play a game while I'm waiting?" Sebastian asked in a plaintive tone.

"Sure, why not?" He shot a quick glance over at Janelle. "That is, if your Aunt Janelle doesn't mind."

"One game," she cautioned, giving Sebastian a stern look. "Just remember, we have to leave for church once the fluid has infused."

"I know," Sebastian said. "Let's play the racecar game!"

Dev didn't mind playing video games, but as they raced around in their respective cars, he couldn't help wondering if it was okay for Sebastian to play outside. Granted he knew that the child probably shouldn't run around too much, considering the fluid that would be dwelling in his abdomen, but surely he could play on a swing-set and maybe play catch.

He made a mental note to ask Janelle since the weather was predicted to be decent over the next few days.

After forty minutes, Janelle returned to the kitchen wearing a knee-length tangerine skirt and matching sweater. He was so distracted by how pretty she looked that he crashed his racecar into the wall.

"I win, I win!" Sebastian shouted.

He blinked, and hoped the back of his neck wasn't too red with embarrassment. "You sure did."

Janelle crossed over to check Sebastian's infusion, seemingly unaware of how she'd managed to cause him to lose the game. "Just a few minutes to go. Then you'll need to get dressed for church."

Sebastian gazed up at him with his wide blue eyes so much like Janelle's. "I want Devon to come to church with us. Please?"

He hesitated and then nodded, unable to refuse the child's simple request. "Okay, I'll come with you. But then I need to get home, okay?"

"Goody!" Sebastian beamed, as if he'd been given a precious gift. Dev shoved his misgivings aside. If going to church with them brightened this kid's day, then it was worth braving the shadows of his past.

Janelle walked him through the rest of the procedure and then sent Sebastian to his room to change.

"You really don't have to go," Janelle murmured once they were alone.

He searched her eyes, trying to read her thoughts. "Would you rather I didn't?"

"Of course not, I'd love for you to attend services with us. I just don't want you to think you have to do every little thing Sebastian asks of you." She hesitated, then added, "I want him to have as normal a life as possible and that means not always getting what he wants."

"I get what you're saying," he agreed. "But it seems like such a little thing to do to make him happy."

She regarded him steadily. "And what about doing what makes you happy?"

He found it difficult to tear his gaze away. Somehow, Janelle seemed to look all the way through him, down to the center of his soul. "I think it's time I put the past to rest, don't you?"

She smiled, her entire face lighting up. "I'm so glad to hear you say that, Devon. God has been waiting for you."

He wasn't so sure, but Sebastian returned just then preventing him from needing to answer. He glanced down at his own attire, knowing he couldn't show up in worn jeans and sweatshirt.

"I'll meet you there, okay?" he said as they walked outside. "I need to change my clothes."

"No problem," she agreed, opening the car door so Sebastian could climb into his booster seat.

Devon slid in behind the wheel and headed home. Without giving himself time to change his mind, he quickly donned a button-down shirt and dress slacks. He couldn't remember the last time he'd dressed nice for a woman.

Not that he was dressing up for Janelle. No, he was only going with them to service because of Sebastian.

Yeah, right. Who was he kidding?

He was going to church with Janelle and Sebastian because he wanted to. For the first time in almost five years, he wasn't allowing sorrowful memories of Debra to hold him back.

In fact, he felt certain that spending time with Janelle and Sebastian would create new memories.

And oddly enough, he found himself looking forward to them.

JANELLE WASN'T sure if Devon would really meet them at church or not. She knew he hadn't been to church in several years, and had been surprised that he'd agreed to come at all.

Obviously he hadn't wanted to disappoint Sebastian. She was troubled by the way her nephew had glommed onto Dev, idolizing him. She told herself it was good for

Sebastian to have a male role model, especially since his father wasn't allowed anywhere near him.

But she couldn't help thinking that Sebastian would be hurt once Dev moved on. She'd heard through the town grape-vine that he was applying for jobs outside of Hope County.

Not that Devon's career choices were any of her business. Still, he'd become so close to Sebastian in such a short time. The child would be devastated once he left.

She really needed to find someone else to babysit Sebastian while she was at work. Dev could help her out for the next couple of days and she had Wednesday off. But then she needed to figure something else out.

The sooner, the better.

"Hi Janelle, hi Sebastian," Merry Crain greeted her cheerfully as they approached. "Looks like you feel much better, young man," she said addressing Sebastian.

"Yep," the little boy nodded. "All better."

"Will you be at work tomorrow?" Merry asked.

"Yes, I have day care set up for Monday and Tuesday," she agreed. "But I still don't have anyone regular lined up."

"Something will work out, you'll see." Merry only worked very part-time because of her own baby. She swapped child care with her sister-in-law, Julie Ryerson.

"I'll keep praying," Janelle said. "Come on, Sebastian, let's go inside."

"We hav'ta wait for Dev," the little boy protested, hanging back.

"Devon Armbruster?" Merry echoed, her eyebrows lifting in surprise. "He hasn't been here in a long time."

"I know, and I'm honestly not sure if he'll make it after all." Janelle glanced down at Sebastian. "How about we go inside and save him a seat?"

Sebastian reluctantly went along with her plan, dragging his feet. Several pews were already full, so she slipped into an empty space near the back.

The organist was playing a soothing hymn and she closed her eyes, letting the music wash over her. Instantly she felt a sense of peace, as if God had lifted each heavy burden off her shoulders.

She silently prayed that God would send her someone to watch over Sebastian so she could return to work. And she prayed that Sebastian would stay healthy, getting the kidney transplant he needed. Lastly, she prayed Devon would find his way back to church and faith.

Sebastian fidgeted in the seat beside her. Her sister hadn't taken him to church, and learning to sit still and listen was a trial for him.

She reached over to put a hand on his shoulder, trying to tell him without words that he needed to sit still.

It took a moment for her to realize that Sebastian had caught a glimpse of Devon striding toward them. Dev looked so handsome in his charcoal gray button down shirt and black pants, her heart squeezed in her chest.

He flashed her a hesitant smile, and then settled in on the other side of Sebastian. She wanted to reach over and clasp his hand reassuringly, but that wasn't possible with her nephew between them.

She was humbled by his presence, especially after he'd been away from church for so long.

As Easter had just passed, the theme of Pastor John's sermon was life after death. She hoped Devon would find the peace he deserved.

It wasn't easy to concentrate on the service, she must have glanced over at Dev at least a dozen times. The parishioners glanced at them curiously, no doubt wondering if they were a new couple.

She hoped Devon wouldn't mind the rumors that would no doubt ripple through their small town. If he noticed their interest in the fact that they were sitting together, he didn't let on.

The service was over far too soon. She knew Devon had to work, so she steeled herself to say goodbye.

"That was nice," he said as they walked back to their respective cars.

She knew she was grinning like an idiot, but couldn't seem to care. "I'm so glad to hear you say that. I thought maybe you'd change your mind about coming."

His brows pulled together in a small frown. "I told you I would," he murmured. "I keep my promises."

"Are you coming to our house?" Sebastian asked, tugging on Devon's belt loop.

"Devon has to work today, remember?" She didn't want Dev to feel as if he had to keep entertaining her nephew. When Sebastian's face fell, she hastened to reassure him. "But he'll be back tomorrow morning to play with you while I'm at work, okay?"

The little boy kicked a rock and shrugged. "Okay," he agreed, his tone mirroring his disappointment.

Dev accompanied them to her car. "How about I give you a call, later?" he suggested. "We'll finalize things for tomorrow."

"Uh, sure, of course," she said, feeling flustered at the thought of Devon calling her. He pulled out his phone and looked at her expectantly. She rattled off her number and he quickly punched it in.

She licked her lips, and told herself to get a grip. Devon was a friend, nothing more. He was sweet enough to help her out of a jam. She had to stop reading something more into his motives.

"Talk to you later," she said, helping Sebastian get into his car seat.

"Will do." Dev waited until she slid behind the wheel to walk over to his truck.

She wrapped her fingers around the steering wheel, biting back the crazy urge to ask him to come over to spend the rest of the day with them.

Ridiculous since she had to make phone calls to possible babysitters anyway.

It didn't take long to drive back to her townhouse, but as she approached she noticed there was a silver sedan parked on the opposite side of the street, directly across from the townhouse.

The same one Devon had noticed last night?

She lifted a hand to shield the sun, trying to see the plate number. But the vehicle abruptly pulled away from the curb, tires screeching as the driver took off.

Her heart leaped into her throat as she pressed hard on the accelerator.

This time, he wasn't going to get away!

6

Janelle was all too aware of the fact that she had Sebastian in the car with her as she tried to close the gap between them.

If only she could get the license plate number!

The silver sedan flew past a stop sign, and Edna Cole, one of the elderly women from their church, lifted a fist and shook it at the vehicle.

Janelle stopped and tapped the steering wheel impatiently as the elderly woman strolled across the street heading toward Rose's café. When the cross walk was clear, she pushed the accelerator, narrowing her gaze as she scanned the area for the silver car.

Her shoulders slumped in defeat when she realized it was gone. No doubt, the driver had taken advantage of her delay at the stop sign to disappear.

With a heavy sigh, she turned around in the parking lot of Pete's Pub and made her way back to the townhouse. When she pulled into the driveway, she was shocked to discover Devon was waiting for them.

"Where did you go?" he asked, as she slid out from behind the wheel.

She hesitated, debating whether or not to tell him. She suspected he wouldn't be happy with her, then again, it wasn't as if they'd been in any danger.

"I saw a silver sedan parked across the street, so I tried to follow." She opened the back passenger door, allowing Sebastian to scramble out.

"You, *what*?" he practically shouted.

"I just wanted to get the license plate number," she said defensively. "But he blew past the stop sign, and I had to wait for Ms. Edna to cross the street, so I lost him."

Dev stared at her for several long moments and she shifted restlessly beneath his glare. "Janelle, please don't do something like that again," he finally said in a soft tone. "You have no idea who that guy is or what he wants. I promise I'll keep an eye on things for you, okay?"

She nodded, but tilted her chin stubbornly. "I know you will, but it is broad daylight on a Sunday afternoon so I highly doubt we were in any real danger."

"Maybe not, but I'd rather you didn't take any unnecessary chances."

Okay, he did have a point. After all, Sebastian had already lost his mother; the poor kid didn't have anyone else in the world but her. "What are you doing here?" she asked, changing the subject.

He rubbed the back of his neck, giving her the impression he was a bit embarrassed. "I just stopped by to practice Sebastian's exchange one more time. You mentioned that he gets one in the early afternoon."

"That's true." She was touched by the fact that Devon was taking his role in performing Sebastian's exchanges seriously. "But we have plenty of time before it's due, so there's no need to hang out here the entire time if you have something else to do."

He hesitated and shrugged. "Nothing more important than this. But I do have a question for you, is Sebastian allowed to play outside?"

She glanced down at her surrogate son. "Yes, he can play outside, as long as he's careful. Running is difficult for him and I wouldn't want him to fall down and injure himself."

"I totally understand, but I was thinking we could maybe walk to the park and swing on the play set." His earnest gaze met hers. "I promise to be careful with him."

Janelle gave herself a mental shake, knowing that she was being over-protective to always think of the worst case scenario. "I trust you, Devon. If you want to walk down to the park with Sebastian I'm fine with that. And I forgot to mention that Sebastian goes to pre-school in the morning, so you'll have to drop him off there after his exchange, around eight-thirty, and then pick him up by eleven-thirty. But that would give you time to head over to the park in the afternoon."

"Great," he said with a relieved smile. "If the weather is nice, we'll give it a try."

Dev's smile transformed his features, making him even more attractive. She tore her gaze away from him with an effort. "Well, looks as if you have everything planned out for tomorrow, then."

"Come on, Dev," Sebastian said, tugging on Devon's slacks. "You said we could play a game."

"We have to check with your Aunt Janelle, first," Devon reminded him.

"Puleeze, Nana," Sebastian begged, his wide blue eyes imploring her to agree.

"All right," she relented. "I have a few phone calls to

make anyway." She was determined to think positively about her chances of securing reliable daycare for Sebastian.

Sebastian let out a whoop of joy, waiting as Janelle unlocked the door before dragging Devon inside the townhouse.

She pulled out a crumpled slip of paper from her purse with a list of names and phone numbers of potential babysitters. One teenage girl in particular had just finished a nursing assistant program and was looking for a part time job. Janelle knew Tina Jamison would be in school during the morning hours, but maybe she could take care of watching Sebastian on the weekends.

Every little bit would help.

But after several calls, she began to lose hope. Tina's mother had promised to pass on the message, but everyone else she spoke to had declined, too afraid of doing the peritoneal dialysis exchanges. One of the older women, Alice, who was a retired nurse hadn't been home, so Janelle had left a message.

She set aside her phone with a sigh and dropped her head into her hands, fighting a wave of despair.

She'd prayed during church, and did so again now.

Dear Lord, please, please help me find a way to provide for Sebastian!

DEV TRIED to concentrate on the game, but he couldn't help overhearing Janelle's failed attempts to line up a babysitter for Sebastian.

Her dejected tone shot straight to his heart and it was all he could do to prevent himself from tossing the controller aside to go over and gather her into his arms.

He forced himself to stay where he was, since he knew that it wouldn't be fair to act on his attraction to her. Especially since staying in Crystal Lake wasn't part of his plan.

But he couldn't deny the need to give her a shoulder to lean on. For her sake? Or his?

Giving himself a mental shake, he tried to think of anyone he knew who might be willing to help out. Getting someone with medical background would be nice, but it wasn't a necessity. Parents without medical background had to learn how to do this kind of thing.

To be fair, he understood the hesitation to take on something as important as performing the child's peritoneal dialysis treatments. He wasn't exactly oozing confidence at the thought of doing them, either.

"Finish up your game," Janelle said, interrupting his thoughts. "We have to get ready to do your exchange."

"No! Don't wanna!" Sebastian argued, his gaze never wavering from the television screen.

Devon hit the pause button, stopping the game. "That's not a nice way to talk to your Aunt," he said mildly.

Sebastian glanced over at Devon, his lower lip trembling. "None of the other kid's hav'ta get exchanges."

His heart squeezed painfully in his chest. What on earth could he say to that? "I know, champ, but you were the one who told me that they didn't hurt, right?"

Sebastian stared down at the controller in his hand. "Right," he mumbled.

Janelle crossed over and dropped onto the sofa beside the child. "Honey, you and I talked about this, remember? We're going to keep praying that God will give you a kidney transplant so that you won't need these exchanges anymore. But until then, this is the best way to keep you healthy so you can play with your friends."

"I know." Sebastian turned and burrowed into Janelle, seeking comfort. She pulled him closer and pressed a kiss to the stop of his head.

Devon couldn't tear his gaze away from the pair, despite how much they reminded him of everything he'd lost. During church services he'd tried to take comfort in the fact that Debra was up in heaven with their unborn child, but it hadn't been easy to let go of the anger at the senselessness of her death.

Why hadn't God spared her life? Why had He taken her away? Dev knew that Janelle would say this was all part of God's master plan, but he wasn't entirely convinced.

Although it had occurred to him that it was possible God wanted him to follow in Steven's footsteps, doing something important to make a difference in the world.

"Ready to do your exchange now?" Janelle asked softly.

Sebastian's head bobbed up and down.

"Great. Stretch out on the sofa and let's see if Dev can remember all the steps."

He groaned. "A test? You're making this a test?"

Sebastian glanced up with a reluctant smile, getting into the spirit of things. "Are you ready?"

"Sure," he said, infusing confidence in his tone. It didn't take him long to set the catheter to drain, that was the easy part. He studied the supplies, trying to remember everything he'd need. He glanced over toward Janelle. "He drains for a half-hour, right?"

"Right."

He played another game with Sebastian while they waited, keeping an eye on the clock. Then he washed his hands again, and began the process of disconnecting the drainage bag. He clamped the open end, then set it aside so he could begin the new infusion. This time wasn't nearly as stressful, and when he finished, he felt a surge of satisfaction. "All set."

"Nice job," Janelle praised him. "You were awesome."

He grinned like a fool, then carried the old bag into the bathroom to dispose of the contents in the toilet. After disposing of the used equipment, he washed his hands again.

"I don't think these hands have ever been so clean," he joked upon returning to the living room.

"Tell me about it, you have no idea how many times I wash my hands at work."

He could well imagine. When he glanced at the clock, he winced. "Listen, I have to run or I'll be late for work."

"I completely understand," Janelle said, rising to her feet. "I'll finish up the exchange, no problem."

He felt guilty for leaving before it was finished, but didn't have much choice. "All right, then. I'll call you later."

"Sounds good." Janelle walked with him to the front door and he noticed she gave a quick glance outside to make sure there were no cars lingering in the street.

"Try not to worry, okay? I'll drive by every hour to check on you."

"Okay, thanks again, for everything."

He didn't want to leave, but forced himself to turn and walk away, her citrusy scent staying with him even after he changed into his uniform.

During roll call, he expected to hear about more robberies, but there was no mention of anything suspicious. In fact, it appeared that other than breaking up a drunk and disorderly and handing out a couple of speeding tickets, nothing much had happened on the previous shift.

Dev knew he should be glad there wasn't a lot of crime in Hope County, especially in the downtown area of Crystal

Lake, but all this proved to him was that he was right to have put in his application at all the big city police departments. He absolutely needed to do something more important with his life than driving around small town, Wisconsin.

Although for some reason the thought of leaving Janelle and Sebastian behind bothered him.

Far more than it should.

JANELLE DIDN'T SLEEP well that night. Not because she was afraid of the silver car, but because she was anxious about leaving Sebastian alone with Devon to return to work.

She loved her job in the ER, and knew Dev was more than capable of doing Sebastian's exchanges. However, she still tossed and turned, waking up to every little noise and glaring at the clock as she ticked off one hour at a time.

At five o'clock in the morning, she gave up trying to sleep. She jumped in the shower and quickly dressed in her forest green scrubs. She pulled her hair back into a pony tail, mostly to keep it out of the way. A patient had once grabbed her by the hair, yanking hard enough to bring tears to her eyes. Not an experience she cared to repeat.

She brewed a pot of coffee and then decided to make breakfast, figuring it was the least she could do for Devon. She owed him far more than she could ever repay, considering he was giving up his two days off to babysit her son.

Her son.

She loved Sebastian more than she thought possible. She smiled as she mixed pancake batter. Hard to believe how much her life had changed in the last month.

For the better.

Granted she still had obstacles to overcome, the largest one being finding a babysitter, but despite the trials she and

Sebastian had been through, she wouldn't give him up for anything.

She poured round circles on the electric griddle and then sipped her coffee as she kept an eye on the pancakes. Glancing at her watch, she wondered if Sebastian would wake up before she had to leave.

The pancakes didn't take long to cook and she stacked them on a plate and covered them with a clean dishtowel to help keep them warm. At six fifteen, there was a soft knock at the door and her heart leapt with anticipation.

Ridiculous, she admonished herself, smoothing her hands over her scrubs before heading over to answer the door. Devon was only here out of kindness, nothing more.

"Good morning," he said, his low husky voice sending a fission of awareness tingling down her spine. He looked amazing, and smelled even better. His dark hair damp from a recent shower and the woodsy scent of his aftershave made her long for something she dared not name.

"Good morning," she responded, striving for a light-hearted tone. "I just finished making breakfast."

"You didn't have to do that," he protested as he crossed the threshold. He sniffed the air and grinned. "Pancakes. Let me guess, another of Sebastian's favorites."

She chuckled. "Of course. I should mention that I have been keeping him on a low salt diet because of his kidneys so that's the only reason I haven't made ham, bacon or sausages for you."

"Am I complaining?" he asked with an arched brow.

"No, you haven't." But Lane had, bitterly. Just another reason she should have gotten rid of him sooner. "Coffee?" she offered, as they walked into the kitchen.

"Sure." He glanced around in surprise. "Sebastian isn't up yet?"

"No, but if he's not awake by six forty-five, you'll need to go in and start draining his catheter. The entire process takes a good ninety minutes."

"Okay, no problem."

She finished her coffee and then set her mug in the sink, feeling self-conscious under his intense gaze. "I'm going to head into work early, if that's okay. You have my cell number, right?" He nodded. "Call me if you have any questions."

"I will," he assured her. "Don't worry, I can handle this."

"I know. Thank you for doing this, I'm not sure how I'll ever repay you."

"No need to repay me," he quickly interjected. "This is what friends are for."

Friends. The word shouldn't have made her depressed. She slipped her purse over her shoulder and headed outside, shoving aside a wave of guilt.

Sebastian and Devon would be fine. She had patients to take care of.

DEVON MANAGED to do Sebastian's exchange, feed him breakfast, get him dressed, and dropped off at pre-school with one minute to spare.

He nearly collapsed in his truck, wondering how on earth Janelle had coped with this all by herself.

Three hours of free time didn't seem like much, but he knew he couldn't afford to waste a minute. He dashed home, threw in a load of laundry and then paid a few bills and balanced his checkbook. Small tasks, but necessary if he was going to spend the afternoon playing babysitter. Two loads of laundry later, he estimated he'd have just enough time to stop at the grocery store for a few basic essentials before he was scheduled to pick Sebastian up again.

He was feeling pretty confident when he arrived at the pre-school with five minutes to spare. So far, so good.

Sebastian came outside with several other boys, and he was glad the kids seemed to accept him as one of their own. Sebastian's face puckered in a frown, but then he noticed Dev and broke into a relieved smile.

"Hey, champ, how was school today?" he asked as he helped Sebastian climb up into his booster seat.

"Good," the boy answered. "Joey's mom is going to take him to the park after lunch, can we go too?"

"Yes, as long as you take your medicine and do your exchange without argument."

Sebastian wrinkled his nose at the medicine, but once they were back at Janelle's townhouse, he swallowed the antibiotic without complaint.

He made Sebastian a grilled cheese sandwich for lunch and then focused on doing the exchange. Dev thought it would be easier without Janelle watching over his shoulder, but he was so afraid of missing a step, or contaminating something, that he kept double checking his work.

"There, all finished," he said in relief. "Once the fluid is in, we'll head over to the park."

"Goody," Sebastian said on a wide yawn.

"Rest for a bit before we go," he suggested. "I have to clean up the kitchen."

The fact that Sebastian didn't put up a fight proved the boy was truly tuckered out. Janelle hadn't said anything about the boy needing a nap, but maybe she assumed he'd know that?

Sebastian dozed in front of the television, but when Dev crossed over to disconnect the bag, his eyes popped open. "Is it time to go to the park?"

He had to suppress a laugh. "Yes, we can go now."

The park wasn't far away, and Dev was glad to see there were other kids playing there, too. Sebastian ran over to meet with his friend Joey.

Dev swept a glance over the area, searching for the silver sedan but didn't see anything. Last night, he hadn't seen the vehicle, either.

The boys played on the swing set and then ran over to the small merry-go-round. "Give us a push, Dev," Sebastian shouted.

He did as they asked, putting a little muscle into it. The merry-go-round spun in a circle and the boys squealed in glee.

"Again! Do it again!"

He spun them around again, but suddenly Sebastian went flying backward, landing on the grass with a thud, and letting out a high-pitched scream.

Dev rushed over, his heart thundering with fear. What if he'd hurt Sebastian?

Janelle would never forgive him.

He'd never forgive himself.

7

Janelle's shift flew past, one minute she was worried about how Devon was doing with Sebastian, the next she was focused on a steady stream of patients coming in through the ER.

A glance at her watch confirmed that it was well past lunch time, and since there seemed to be a break in the action, she decided to take advantage of the moment to get a bite to eat.

And to call Devon.

She grabbed a sandwich from the cafeteria and took it back upstairs to the ER break room. She took a bite while scrolling through her contact list. Then she switched over to her recent calls.

Dev had called her the night before to finalize things and to check in on her. She found his number and added him to her contact list before she pushed the button.

The phone rang several times before his voice mail message came on. She frowned and asked that he call her back.

Weird, she thought, as she took another bite. Maybe he

was at the park, playing with Sebastian and hadn't heard his phone. Although surely he would have expected her to call?

Then again, maybe not. She'd told him she trusted him. Which she did. And she might have caught them in the middle of a game.

She finished her lunch, and then sighed when she was notified of a new arrival. Ten minutes to eat was better than nothing, so she tossed the wrapper in the garbage and headed back out to the arena.

"Janelle, your patient is in room three," Eve informed her.

She nodded and crossed over. When she pushed back the privacy curtain, her heart leapt into her throat when she saw Dev standing beside Sebastian who was lying on a gurney.

"What happened?" she asked, crossing over to put a hand on Sebastian's forehead. "Is he sick?"

Devon's face was full of anguish. "I spun him on the merry-go-round and he fell off. I'm so sorry, it's totally my fault."

For a moment the urge to lash out at him was strong, and she swallowed the harsh words with an effort. "It's okay," she said with a strained smile. "Sebastian? Can you tell me what hurts?"

"My tummy," he whimpered.

She tried to control her shaking fingers as she lifted his shirt and examined his abdomen. The catheter site looked fine, clean, dry and intact. He didn't have any obvious bruises or contusions that she could see, although it was possible they would show up later. She glanced up at Devon. "Did he land on his stomach?"

"No, he landed on his backside."

She was relieved by the news. "Okay, I'm sure he'll be fine, but I'll ask Dr. Katy to take a look."

As she moved around to the foot of the gurney, Dev's hand shot out and lightly grasped her arm. "Janelle, I'm truly sorry about this."

He looked so distraught that her initial annoyance faded and she covered his hand with hers. "I don't blame you, Devon. Sebastian is a child, he's going to fall down or get hurt sometimes."

"I pushed them too fast," he insisted. "You warned me to be careful and look what happened."

"Nothing has happened that we know of," she reminded him. "We'll see what Dr. Katy says, but I'm sure he's going to be just fine."

Dev's dark gaze clung to hers, as if seeking reassurance. Finally he released her and nodded. "Okay, send the doc in."

She strode into the arena and swept her gaze over the nurse's station, searching for Dr. Katy's auburn hair. The ER doctor was seated in front of a computer, scowling at the screen. Janelle approached her, wondering what was wrong. "Dr. Katy? Do you have a minute to examine my patient in room three?"

"What?" Dr. Katy glanced up and her expression cleared. "Sure, I'll be right in."

"Anything I can help you with?" Janelle asked, glancing at the computer screen over Katy's shoulder.

"No, just don't like the look of this CT scan on the patient in room eight but I have consulted the neurologist; just waiting for him to get here." Dr. Katy pushed away from the computer desk. "Let's take a look at your patient. What's going on?"

Janelle filled her in on Sebastian's medical history and was glad when Dr. Katy didn't seem too concerned.

When they walked into the room, Devon was sitting next to Sebastian's gurney, smoothing a hand over her son's head.

"Hi Devon," Dr. Katy greeted him. "Is Sebastian your son?"

Dev looked stunned by the question and Janelle quickly spoke up. "No, he's actually my son. I'm his legal guardian, Dev was just helping me out by watching Sebastian today while I was here at work."

"Oh, of course, I should have known. Now that you mention it, I did hear something about you adopting your sister's son." Katy bent over Sebastian. "Hi, my name is Dr. Katy, can I take a peek at your tummy?"

Sebastian nodded and pulled up his t-shirt. Dr. Katy gently palpated his abdomen and glanced over at Janelle. "He's dwelling, right?"

She nodded. "Yes, that's right. He's not scheduled for another exchange until later tonight."

"I think we need to make sure the fluid in his abdomen is clear," Dr. Katy said, stepping back and stripping off her gloves. "So let's get him drained, then we'll get a CT scan. If it looks good, I'll discharge him home."

"Do we need to infuse another bag?" Janelle asked with a frown. She didn't like the idea of skipping an exchange.

"I don't think so, he should really be fine for a couple of hours. Just start his nighttime exchange an hour early."

Janelle nodded and quickly connected the tubing to Sebastian's catheter. She held her breath and released the clamp, hoping, praying there was no blood in the fluid as a sign of trauma.

She could feel Devon's intense gaze, both of them waiting to see what would happen. When the fluid appeared clear, she smiled. "Looks good."

"Yeah." Dev glanced up at her. "I've been praying the whole time that he'd be okay."

She was touched by the fact that he'd prayed for Sebastian, especially considering how he'd kept his distance from church and faith. Maybe yesterday had helped mend that fence. "Me, too. But as you can see, he's fine."

"Can I go home, now?" Sebastian asked. "I wanna play the race car game."

"Not yet, but soon." Janelle glanced up at Devon. "I have a couple of other patients to check on, but I'll be back in a few minutes."

He nodded. "I'm not going anywhere."

She kept busy with her other patients, while Dev accompanied Sebastian to the CT scanner. She wanted to be there for him, but she couldn't just walk away from her patient care responsibilities, either.

When Dr. Katy gave them the all clear, she glanced at her watch, realizing she only had thirty minutes left in her shift. "I can't leave just yet," she told Dev. "But I'll meet you soon, okay?"

"Sure, no problem." Dev looked exhausted, as if the events at the park had taken a toll on him. "We'll play video games while we wait, right Sebastian?"

"Right. And I'll beat you, too."

She smiled at Sebastian's determination, glad to see he was back to his old self. She kept the discharge paperwork for herself, watching as Sebastian skipped beside Dev as they left the ER.

As fast as the beginning part of her shift passed, the last thirty minutes dragged painfully slow. When she finished giving the oncoming nurse a brief report about the patients who were still waiting for their disposition, she hurried to grab her purse out of her locker.

Thankfully, the ride home didn't take long, and for once there was no sign of any silver sedan hanging around. She found Dev and Sebastian playing a game, but was equally shocked to see that there was a large crockpot of beef stew on the counter.

"You made dinner?" She glanced at Dev in surprise.

"I used a low salt recipe so it should be fine for Sebastian," he responded from his spot on the sofa.

She didn't know what to say, certainly she hadn't expected him to cook for her.

For them.

This was how she'd once envisioned her life.

Before Lane had walked out on her.

She told herself not to read anything into Devon's kind gesture. After all, he was probably just returning the favor since she'd cooked breakfast.

Yet she had no idea what to do with the extra time on her hands. Time she'd slotted to prepare dinner.

She ducked into her bedroom to change out of her scrubs into a comfy pair of soft denim jeans and a pull-over T-shirt.

When she returned to the kitchen, Devon was standing at the counter, stirring the stew. He turned when she approached.

"What do you want to do about tomorrow?" he asked in a low voice.

Her stomach sank to the soles of her feet. The way he avoided her gaze made her realize he'd changed his mind about watching Sebastian. She could barely force the words past her constricted throat. "What do you mean?"

"Can you still trust me, after everything that's happened?"

She licked her dry lips. "I'll be honest, Devon, I was

angry at first. But then I realized that this could have happened to anyone."

"But not to you." He finally lifted his gaze to hers.

"I've probably been a little over-protective of him," she admitted. "But what I said to you in the ER was the truth. He's going to run and play with other kids. He's going to fall down and get hurt. You were right to take him to the park to play. He shouldn't spend his days playing video games."

"Do you really mean that?" he asked, his dark brown eyes searching hers.

She couldn't stop herself from stepping closer and putting her hand on his forearm. "Yes, I do. Please don't let what happened today bother you."

"How can I not?" Dev's tone was husky with pent up emotion. "Sebastian could have been seriously injured."

"Yes, but he wasn't."

He pulled her close, wrapping his arms around her. She linked her arms around his waist and rested her head on his shoulder. They stood there for several long moments, drawing strength from each other.

When Dev finally loosened his grip, she stepped away, feeling a bit self-conscious. They were friends, but in the past few days, she was beginning to think of him as something more.

"Thanks for making dinner," she said, desperate to change the subject. "I hope you're planning on staying to eat with us."

He hesitated for a moment before nodding. "Sure, I'd like that."

It was on the tip of her tongue to ask what they were doing, but just then Sebastian called out for Dev, asking if he was going to return to the game.

"Go ahead," she urged, distracted by the ringing of her cell phone. "I have to get this anyway."

Dev headed back into the living room and challenged Sebastian to another game. She picked up her phone, frowning when she didn't recognize the number.

"Hello?"

"Hi this is Alice Beckstrom, returning your call."

Janelle was thrilled to hear from the retired nurse. She explained her situation with Sebastian and asked if there was any possibility she'd be willing to babysit for him, which included performing his peritoneal dialysis exchanges three times a day.

There was a long pause and Janelle's hope deflated like a balloon.

"I know it sounds like a lot," she hastened to fill the silence. "But he goes to preschool in the morning, so it's really not as bad as it sounds."

"How many days a week would you need me?" Alice asked.

She caught her breath, trying to rein in her excitement. "I'm working just part-time hours for now, usually two to three days per week, and every third weekend."

Another long silence. "I don't do weekends."

At this point, she would be willing to take what she could get. "That's okay, I'm hoping a young high-school student who's already a certified nursing assistant will be willing to do them." She took a deep breath and pressed on. "I would really appreciate your considering the position. I have to be able to pay my rent and I'm running out of options."

"All right, then I'll watch your boy two or three days per week. But it's been a long time so I'll need a refresher on how to do his exchanges."

Janelle closed her eyes on a wave of relief, resisting the urge to dance a little jig. "I'm off work on Wednesday, but work again on Thursday. I can show you how to take care of his exchanges on Wednesday if you're willing. I only need you Thursday of this week, and then not again until Monday the following week."

"Wednesday is fine. I'll need directions to your house."

Janelle rattled them off and then disconnected from the call, letting out a heavy sigh of relief. She sank into a kitchen chair, trying to absorb what had just happened.

God had answered her prayers! She had a babysitter for Sebastian. For during the week at least.

She'd have plenty of time to worry about the weekends later.

Suddenly full of energy, she jumped up from the table and began pulling glasses, bowls and silverware out of her cupboards, setting the table. Devon's beef stew smelled delicious and she was acutely aware of how hungry she was.

"Dinner's ready," she called.

"Not yet," Sebastian protested, leaning into a curve as if he were actually riding the race car.

Devon hit the pause button. "Yes, now," he said, firmly. "We can finish the game after dinner."

As much as she was glad to have his support, she couldn't help wondering just how long Dev planned on staying. He had a right to eat the meal he'd cooked, but surely he had other things to do.

Other ways to spend his evening off work.

Her stomach knotted at the thought of Devon dating someone else, even though she knew he didn't belong to her. And after tomorrow, she wouldn't even need his help any more with watching Sebastian.

So why was she feeling depressed by that fact?

She filled their bowls with the steamy stew, and once everyone was seated she clasped her hands together and bowed her head.

"Dear Lord, we thank You so much for this wonderful food and for keeping Sebastian safe today when he fell. Also thank You for answering my prayers for a babysitter. We ask that You continue to show us Your path, Amen."

"Amen," Sebastian said.

She glanced at Devon, surprised at the somber expression on his face.

"You found someone?"

She forced a smile. "Yes, Alice Beckstrom, the retired nurse that Pastor John referred to me. She doesn't want to do weekends, but at least I have part of my problem solved."

"That's great news," he said with an odd lack of enthusiasm.

She nodded and picked up her spoon, wondering what was going on in his mind.

Was it possible Devon would miss spending time with Sebastian?

With her?

8

D evon knew he should be happy for Janelle's having a solution for her babysitting problem. However, he couldn't deny a twinge of regret that she wouldn't need him anymore.

Ridiculous to think that way, this wasn't about him. Both Janelle and Sebastian deserved a break.

"Delicious," Janelle murmured after tasting his stew. "Thank you so much for making dinner. I wasn't expecting you to do that."

"It was really not that big a deal," he said, wishing she wouldn't be so nice to him. The image of Sebastian lying on the ground beside the merry-go-round and the shrillness of his scream were firmly implanted in his memory.

He hadn't prayed that hard since Debra's death.

Cooking dinner had been his feeble attempt to repay her. It was the least he could do.

"Actually, it is a big deal," Janelle countered. She reached across the table and lightly put her hand on his forearm. "You've been so supportive over these past few days, Devon. I'm not sure how I'll ever repay you."

He stared at her slender hand for a moment, aching for something he didn't dare name, then dragged his gaze to her face. "You supported me the night I was shot, Janelle," he managed. "So how about we just consider ourselves even?"

The smile that bloomed across her features made his breath catch in his throat. "Okay, then. It's a deal."

He nodded and began to eat. The stew wasn't half bad, and he was glad to see Sebastian and Janelle both seemed to like it too.

"Have you heard any news from Zack about the break in?" he asked.

Janelle scowled and shook her head. "No, but I'm sure these things take time."

They did, but he thought Zack would have tried to put a rush on the fingerprints at least. Although the robbery had been discovered on Saturday, the evidence was probably only first being processed today.

"Everything can be replaced," Janelle said with a shrug. Then her expression clouded over. "Except for Lisa's ring."

"I can check out some of the pawn shops and jewelry shops in the area," he volunteered.

She looked up at him in surprise. "Won't Zack do that?"

"Maybe," he acknowledged. "But it won't hurt to have both of us making phone calls."

"I'd appreciate that," she said softly.

Dev couldn't help thinking he'd do anything to make her happy, but then pulled himself up short. Wait a minute, what was he thinking? They were friends.

Good friends. Helping each other out in a jam.

So why did he have the insane urge to kiss her?

Devon tried to push the troublesome thoughts out of his mind, but it wasn't easy. When they finished dinner, Janelle insisted on cleaning up. He decided he should head home, after all, he'd be back in the morning.

"I'll see you tomorrow, Janelle. Same time, right?"

"Right."

"Noooo," Sebastian wailed. "Don't go, Dev. Don't go!"

He was surprised when the little boy wrapped his arms around his legs, in a meager attempt to keep him from leaving.

"Hey, champ, I need to get going, but I'll be back in the morning, okay?"

"Can't you stay and play wif me? Puleeze?"

"Sebastian," Janelle said in a stern, warning tone. "That's enough. You need to get your jammies on, Dr. Katy said we need to do your exchange an hour earlier tonight."

"Don't wanna!" Sebastian abruptly let go of his legs and ran down the hall toward his bedroom. The door slammed shut behind him.

"I can stay for a little while," Devon began, but Janelle quickly interrupted.

"No, the sooner Sebastian realizes that he can't get everything he wants, the better."

She was probably right, what did he know about raising a child? Not much. But he was still hesitant to leave. "Are you sure?"

"Yes, I'm sure," she said firmly. "He's tired, but he'll get over being upset soon enough." She made her way over to the front door, leaving him little choice but to follow. "See you in the morning."

"I'll be here." He couldn't resist the urge to touch her, so he gave her a quick hug, and then left the townhouse. He could feel her gaze on his back as he walked to his truck.

The minute he returned home, he booted up his

computer and did a search on the closest jewelry stores that advertised buying gold.

He picked up his mobile phone and began dialing, determined to find Janelle's missing ring. He'd try the jewelry stores first, as they were closer, then move on to the pawn shops, most of which were located in either Madison or Milwaukee.

As he worked, he was all too aware that his need to make Janelle happy came from a personal need, rather than a professional one.

THE NEXT MORNING, Janelle wasn't up quite as early, so she wasn't able to make breakfast. Devon didn't seem to mind, but she still felt a bit guilty for rushing out and leaving him to face Sebastian's exchange alone.

This time, there were no crises to worry about. Her shift dragged by slowly, but when she checked in with Devon he assured her everything was fine.

A heart attack victim came in through the ER right before shift change, so she ended up staying a little later than usual to help get the patient settled. When she was free to leave, she sent Dev a quick text telling him she was on her way home.

The ride home didn't take long, but when she walked into the townhouse, there was no sign of Sebastian or Devon. She frowned, her heart racing. Had they gone to the park again?

Then she heard Sebastian giggle, and realized the patio door was open, allowing a cool breeze to wash in through the screen. Dev and Sebastian were outside in the back yard, standing a few feet apart on the grassy area over-looking the lake. She stood in front of the patio doors for a moment, watching as Devon gently tossed a baseball to Sebastian, who tried to catch it in a too big leather baseball glove.

"That's it, good job," Dev was saying.

Sebastian glowed under his praise and threw the ball back in Devon's direction. Dev did a good job of leaping to the side to catch the ball.

For a moment she simply watched them, loving the way Devon was so patient with Sebastian, the way a father should be with his son.

Would Devon find someone else to marry one day? Would he have a family of his own? The thought was bittersweet.

"Nana!" Sebastian caught sight of her in the doorway. "We're playing catch!"

"I see that," she said with a smile.

The next ball Devon lobbed at Sebastian he dropped, but the one after that managed to land awkwardly in his glove. Sebastian threw it back at Devon with more force causing Dev to scramble in order to prevent it from hitting the side of the house.

Janelle tried not to wince. "Good catch," she said to Dev.

He grinned, looking younger and somehow more carefree. "Sebastian is keeping me on my toes."

"Clearly," she said in a dry tone. "Thanks for staying, sorry I had to work late."

"No problem. Are you hungry? I was planning to cook burgers and brats on the grill for dinner."

Janelle knew that Sebastian was already becoming too attached to Devon, but at the same time, she enjoyed spending time with him. Probably a little too much. "Sure, if you don't mind."

"Of course not, or I wouldn't have offered."

"Throw me the ball, Dev," Sebastian said, hitting the center of his glove like some pro baseball player.

Janelle stepped back from the doorway, and turned to head into her room. She changed out of her scrubs then returned to the kitchen, checking to see if she had enough veggies in the fridge to make a salad to go with the burgers and brats.

The fact that this was their last night together wasn't lost on her as she shredded lettuce and chopped up tomatoes. Of course she could always invite Devon over for a meal, but that would be difficult since he worked second shift, while she primarily worked dayshift.

Crazy to worry about when she'd see Devon again, considering that up until four days ago, she'd hardly spent any time with him. How was it that he'd become such a fixture in their lives in just a few days?

Dating Lane for a year hadn't given her the same feeling of closeness that she experienced now with Devon.

As if on cue, Dev opened the screen door of the patio and came inside. "Looks great," he said, eyeing the salad bowl.

"I'm trying to get Sebastian to like vegetables as much as he likes macaroni and cheese," she said dryly. "I don't think my sister was big on healthy cooking."

Dev snatched a cucumber, drawing his hand away quickly when she playfully swatted it. "You don't talk about her much."

She shrugged. "Don't get me wrong, I loved Lisa, but she didn't always make the best choices. Like living with Grant and getting pregnant. But she was getting on the right track after Sebastian was born."

"I didn't mean to dredge up painful memories," he said.

She sent him a sideways glance. "We both have painful memories, don't we?"

He nodded and turned away, to gaze out through the patio doors. She sensed he wasn't quite ready to talk about the loss of his fiancée, and she didn't blame him.

Was that the reason he wanted to move out of Crystal Lake? Her heart squeezed in her chest and she realized just how sad she would be to see him go.

"How's the job hunt going?" she asked, striving for a casual tone.

He swung toward her in surprise. "How did you know about that?"

She arched a brow. "Seriously?"

He rolled his eyes toward the ceiling. "Let me guess, Josie said something to you."

Her lips twitched in a smile. "Bingo."

"How does she find this stuff out?" he asked, truly baffled. "It's not like I told very many people about my plan."

"She eavesdrops on her customer's conversations," she responded with a smile. "She mentioned overhearing Sheriff Torretti making a comment about getting a reference call about you."

"Really?" Devon's eyes widened. "He got a reference call?"

"According to Josie. She thinks you can't bear to live here anymore because of all the reminders about your fiancée."

"That's not the reason," he protested. "It's just—I feel the need to do something more with my life. Something important. Truly making a difference."

She wanted to point out that he was making a difference to her and Sebastian, but knew that wasn't what he was talking about. "I understand," she said, putting the last of the cucumbers into the salad bowl.

"You do?"

She nodded and opened the fridge and placed the salad bowl inside. "I used to work at the big level one trauma center in Madison for the same reason. But eventually I realized that seeing nameless faces day in and day out wasn't really what I wanted. Even at church I didn't necessarily feel as if I truly belonged. I wanted a sense of community. The minute I arrived in Crystal Lake, I knew this was home."

Devon didn't say anything in response to that, so she finished cleaning up the cutting board and then crossed over to stand next to him in front of the patio doors. "What's Sebastian up to?" she asked, changing the subject.

"Practicing," Dev said with a smile. He was so close she could breathe in the woodsy scent of his aftershave. "I taught him to toss the ball up in the air and practice catching it."

"Hmm, maybe I should get him a smaller glove," she said, watching as Sebastian dropped more balls than he managed to catch. "That one seems way too big."

"I think I have one of my nephew's gloves somewhere so don't buy anything until I have a chance to search the basement."

She was touched by his willingness to loan his nephews things to Sebastian. Of course, the fact that she'd told him all about her money problems was likely a factor, too. "Okay, thanks. But there's no rush, I've taken up more than enough of your free time."

He turned to look down at her with his deep brown eyes. She caught her breath, unable to tear her gaze away. He lifted his hand and lightly brushed a stray strand of hair off her cheek. "I like spending my free time with you," he said in a low voice.

She parted her lips, trying to come up with some sort

of response, not easy when all she could think of was kissing him. And then he slowly bent his head toward her, giving her plenty of time to back away if she were so inclined.

She wasn't.

Instead she found herself leaning forward, meeting him halfway. The moment his mouth covered hers, every logical thought slid right out of her brain. He tasted amazing, like chocolate and peppermint rolled into one.

When Devon deepened the kiss, she found herself clinging to his broad shoulders, drowning in sensation. Somewhere nearby, an odd buzzing sound nagged at her, but she ignored it.

Devon lifted his mouth from hers, breathing heavily. "I think that's your phone," he said.

She didn't want to let go, but of course, the buzzing continued. Remembering she'd set the device on vibrate, she forced herself to release him.

Her legs were shaky as she crossed over to the kitchen table. The name on the screen was Zack Crain, so she picked it up and pushed the talk button. "Hello, Zack."

"Did I catch you at a bad time?" he asked.

Yes, she wanted to shout, but of course she didn't. She glanced over at Devon, who stood with his shoulder propped against the doorway, watching her. "Just getting ready for dinner," she said, sidestepping his question. "Why? Did you find something out about the robbery?"

"Actually, we do have a clue, but is Devon there? Apparently he's the one who did most of the work."

Color rushed into her cheeks. "Um, yeah, he's here. Do you want to talk to him?"

"No, that's not necessary, but tell him thanks for the tip."

"Here, I'll put you on speaker," she said, taking the

phone from her ear to push the button. "Go ahead, Devon's here, too."

Devon crossed over to stand next to the phone. "Hey Zack, what did you find out?"

"Did you call and leave a message at Gretchen's Goldsmith shop about a ruby ring?" Zack asked.

"Yes, I called Gretchen's among others," Devon admitted.

Janelle's heart leaped in her chest. "Lisa's ring? Did you find it?"

"The owner of the goldsmith shop let us know she did buy a gold ring with a red stone," Zack said. "But don't get too excited, we don't know for sure it's the same ring."

"Do you have a picture of it?" Janelle asked excitedly.

"Yeah, I can e-mail it to you."

"Wait, I don't have a computer, remember?" Janelle said. "The thief took that, too. Can you text the photo to me?"

"Send it to both of us," Devon spoke up.

"Okay, here it comes."

Devon's phone chirped and he quickly pressed on the text button to see what Zack had sent. He maneuvered the photo so it was larger in size and then turned the phone to show her. "Is this the ring?" he asked.

She stared in shock at the photograph. "Yes, that's Lisa's ring," she said in a choked voice.

"Did you hear that?" Dev asked Zack. "Janelle has positively identified the ring. Did the owner give you a description of the guy who sold it?"

"She did, said he was tall and skinny, with dirty blond hair and a scruffy beard. He wore a green T-Shirt and worn blue jeans that appeared to be a size too large on him. Any idea who he might be?" Zack asked.

Janelle tried to picture the man, but honestly that

description could have been anyone. "I'm sorry, but I can't think of anyone who matches that description."

There was a long silence. "Okay, don't worry about it, I'm sure we'll find him eventually," Zack assured her.

She nodded, wishing she could be so sure. When Zack disconnected from the call, she saw that Devon was pulling his car keys out of his pocket. "Where are you going?"

"We're going to get Lisa's ring back." Dev turned and called through the patio doors to Sebastian. "Come on, Sebastian, we're going for a ride."

She wanted to protest, first because she didn't have any spare money to buy Lisa's ring back, and second she had no idea how long it would take. She needed to get back in time to do Sebastian's exchange.

But when Devon held out his hand, she found herself taking it, liking the way his warm fingers gently cradled hers.

She found herself agreeing with his impromptu plan. "Let's go."

9

Devon did his best to concentrate on driving, but his mind kept going back to reliving their kiss. He had no idea why he'd kissed Janelle, but there was no denying she'd kissed him back, sending sparks of electricity zipping along his nerve endings.

He hadn't felt this level of attraction for any woman in a long time. Not since Debra.

And unfortunately the memories of his former fiancée were growing distant, which made him feel bad.

But not enough to make him regret kissing Janelle. And not enough to think about how much he'd like to kiss her again.

"Just give me a minute to pack some supplies," Janelle said, before rushing toward Sebastian's bedroom.

Supplies? He belatedly remembered Sebastian's need for dialysis. He hesitated, wondering if he should offer to go and pick up her sister's ring alone. No reason to drag Janelle and Sebastian along.

When she returned with a small backpack full of

supplies, he put a hand on her arm. "Why don't you and Sebastian stay here? I'll get the ring and bring it to you."

Indecision flashed across her features, but then she shook her head. "No, I'd like to come. And I'm only dragging all this stuff along just in case. We'll probably be back in plenty of time."

He relented. "Okay, is there anything else you need?"

"Nope, all set. Well, except for Sebastian."

He glanced through the patio doors. "Store that stuff in the car, I'll get him."

Janelle nodded, and he crossed over to the sliding doors. "Sebastian? Come inside, we're getting ready to go for a ride."

The little boy didn't waste any time tossing aside his baseball and glove.

"Oh, no. You need to bring your things inside," Devon instructed.

Sebastian let out a heavy sigh, but did as he was told. Within five minutes, the boy was tucked into the booster seat and they were on the road, heading for the interstate.

Dev glanced at Janelle. "Are you sure that description didn't sound familiar?"

She pursed her lips and then lifted her shoulders in a helpless shrug. "Not one bit. I've been trying to go through the teenagers I happen to know around town, but that description doesn't fit."

He wasn't so sure the burglar was a kid from town, but there was no point in pushing the issue. Hopefully, the goldsmith shop would have security cameras that would give them a decent angle. If the guy had been smart enough to avoid them, maybe the owner would agree to work with a police artist to create a sketch.

And why were the fingerprints taking so long? They

should have had something back by now. Unless of course the perp wasn't in the system.

His truck ate up the miles as Janelle and Sebastian sang nursery rhymes. Twenty minutes later, he pulled up in front of Gretchen's Goldsmith.

"Are you ready?" he asked Janelle, as she unbuckled her seatbelt.

"Absolutely." She hopped down from the truck and reached up to get Sebastian.

Inside the shop there were rows and rows of glass cases containing all kinds of jewelry. It was a nice place, looked as if they sold high end jewelry. Odd that the robber would choose a nice place to sell the gold ring.

Unless he sold it to someone else, first? The possibility of this being a dead end made him frown.

A woman with an athletic build and weathered skin came out of the back room to greet them. "Janelle Larson?"

"That's me," Janelle said, stepping forward.

The woman smiled. "My name is Gretchen, I understand this is your ring?"

Janelle glanced at the ring, then down at Sebastian. "Actually, it belonged to my sister, Sebastian's mother. It's the only thing of value she possessed and I was saving it for her son."

Gretchen's expression softened. "That's very nice." She held out the ring. "Here, take it."

Janelle didn't move, so Dev stepped forward, reaching for his wallet. "How much did you pay for it?"

Gretchen waved him away. "Really not that much, and I wouldn't have given that guy any money at all if I had known it was stolen."

Janelle reached for the ring. "At least let me pay what you spent, it's not fair for you to lose money on the deal."

"Don't worry about me, I have insurance. Besides, business has been good. I have no complaints."

Devon was touched by Gretchen's kindness. "Are you sure?"

"Positive, just remember me if you're ever in the market for jewelry." Gretchen's eyes softened as she watched Janelle cradle the ring. "Glad to help out."

"You've been wonderful, thank you," Janelle said, slipping the ruby ring on her right hand.

"Can we take a look at your security cameras?" Dev asked.

"Sure." Gretchen led the way over to her office. She brought up the camera feed and went in reverse to find the guy who'd brought the ring in.

He wore a baseball hat pulled over his hair, and a scruffy beard covered the lower portion of his face. Dev sighed. "Not very useful, but will you save it on a disk?"

"Of course." Gretchen shrugged. "Sorry I couldn't be much help."

"You were a huge help," Janelle said, fingering the ring. "Thanks again, for everything."

Devon placed his hand in the small of her back as they headed out to the truck. "So what do you think? Do we have time to stop for dinner? That way, you can do the exchange right when you get home."

"Sounds good," Janelle agreed. "Right Sebastian?"

"Right," the child echoed.

Devon drove toward a family style restaurant, rather than a fast food place, knowing it would be easier to find something lower in salt for Sebastian.

When their food arrived, Janelle folded her hands together and bowed her head. "Thank You, Lord, for providing this food for us and for bringing my sister's ring home. We ask that You continue to keep Sebastian healthy as we follow Your chosen path, Amen."

"Amen," he murmured. When Dev lifted his head, he caught Janelle's gaze and smiled. Praying with her didn't feel awkward or forced. Instead, it felt right.

For the first time, he realized that leaving Janelle and Sebastian behind just to work on some big city police force wouldn't be as easy as he'd once thought.

He didn't want to leave her at all.

JANELLE WAS RELIEVED they'd made it back home in time to do Sebastian's exchange. Devon hung around for a while, but once Sebastian was tucked into bed, he made his way to the front door. She reluctantly followed him.

"Thanks again, Dev."

He stared down at her for a long minute, and she held her breath, hoping he might kiss her again.

But he didn't. "I'm glad you were able to get your sister's ring back," he said in a low, husky tone.

"Me, too. It was nice of Gretchen to just give it to me."

He nodded and rubbed the back of his neck. "Take care, Janelle. Let me know if you need anything."

She curled her fingers into fists to prevent herself from reaching out to him. Obviously, Devon considered their brief kiss a colossal mistake. She forced a smile, trying not to think about how lonely it would be to not have him around. "I will."

He turned away and strode to his car. She watched, waiting for him to turn back. But he slid behind the wheel and backed out of the driveway.

She stepped back inside and closed the door, feeling bereft, even though she knew she had no reason to. Despite how she'd responded to his kiss, it wasn't as if they were dating.

Devon was likely still mourning his fiancée.

And she had a young boy to care for.

Janelle didn't sleep well that night, tossing and turning, imagining that the silver car was parked once again outside her house. Crazy, since she hadn't seen the vehicle in well over twenty-four hours.

The next morning, she performed Sebastian's exchange, then cleaned up the house in preparation for Alice's visit. Janelle didn't know Alice, but when the woman arrived, just after noon, the woman wasn't anything like what she'd imagined.

Alice had a rotund frame and wasn't smiling, in fact she seemed to have a permanent frown etched on her fore-head. Her gray hair was pulled back into a harsh bun, and she moved slowly when Janelle opened the door to let her in.

"Sebastian," Janelle called, trying her best to ignore her misgivings. "Ms. Alice is here."

Sebastian glanced over and then scowled when he saw the retired nurse standing there. "Don't wanna do my exchange," he said, turning his attention back to his game.

Janelle forced a bright smile. "Come on, Sebastian, we need to show Mrs. Alice how to do this."

She feared he'd throw a tantrum, but he tossed aside the controller. "Okay, let's get this over with," he said in a resigned tone.

Janelle was glad to see that Alice at least appeared to be paying attention as she walked through the steps. The woman didn't say much, but after they finished, she reached for her purse.

"What time tomorrow?" she asked in an abrupt tone.

"I have to be at work by seven, so if you could get here by six-thirty that would be great."

"Okay, fine. I'll see you then." Alice clomped her way back toward the door.

Janelle told herself not to panic at her abrupt departure, after all, the woman was a nurse. Surely she'd do fine.

"Where's Dev?" Sebastian asked a few minutes later. "I don't like her, I want Dev."

Oh boy, this was exactly what she was afraid of. Sebastian had already grown too attached to Devon Armbruster.

And if she were honest, she'd admit she'd grown attached to him, too.

"He's working as a police officer," she reminded Sebastian. "Mrs. Alice is going to be your babysitter from now on."

Sebastian's face crumpled. "No! Don't want Mrs. Alice! She smells funny!"

Since the scent of mothballs had clung to Alice's badly wrinkled clothes, she couldn't exactly argue with him. "I'm sorry, Sebastian, but Devon has to work."

He thrust out his lower lip. "Then you stay home with me."

A wave of guilt hit her hard. "I can't, I have to work, too."

"NOOOO!" Sebastian screeched in a voice loud enough to shatter ear drums.

"Stop it," she shouted in a sharp tone. "That's enough. Go to your room."

He scrambled off the sofa, tears rolling down his chubby cheeks and ran into his bedroom, slamming the door loudly behind him.

Janelle collapsed on the edge of a kitchen chair, burying her face in her hands. She probably could have handled that better. Thankfully, no one was renting the townhouse next door. She could only hope that no one else had heard the shouting match, the last thing she needed was an unexpected visit from child protective services.

The worst part of it all, was that she couldn't even blame Sebastian for not liking Alice. Truthfully, she hadn't been overly thrilled with the woman's demeanor, either. She'd seemed so nice over the phone, but in person, ugh. But what could she do? The rent was due in just three weeks, and she'd be lucky if her paycheck covered the amount.

The urge to call and cry on Devon's shoulder was strong, but somehow she managed to hold back. He didn't need to listen to her sob story when he was busy getting ready for his shift. Besides, there really wasn't anything he could do.

No, this was one mess she had to deal with alone.

Sebastian's wails grew louder to the point she covered her ears. Then she abruptly pushed away from the kitchen table and let herself out through the patio doors.

The lake was calm just a few boats dotted the water. The sun was out, but it wasn't quite warm enough to swim or ski.

She walked until she couldn't hear Sebastian's crying anymore, stopping at the edge of the lake, in front of the white pier. She drew in a deep breath and let it out slowly, seeking peace.

Lots of kids had temper tantrums, this wasn't Sebastian's first, nor would it likely be his last. She closed her eyes and prayed that the Lord would continue to provide strength and wisdom.

Maybe she needed to keep searching for another babysitter for Sebastian. Obviously she had to work tomorrow, so she'd need to use Alice for that, but then she had another three days off to work on a replacement.

Someone other than Devon.

Although she'd already gone through her entire list, and she still hadn't heard back from Tina, the teenager who'd finished her nursing assistant training, either. She'd had high hopes for Tina, since she could only assume Sebastian would like having a younger woman watching over him.

She sat down on the grass and wrapped her arms around her knees. She'd give Sebastian some time to calm down, and then she'd offer to take him to the park. This was nothing more than a minor setback.

They'd get through this. They had to.

She and Sebastian only had each other.

Janelle forced herself to sit there, gazing at the lake for a full fifteen minutes. When the timeframe was up, she pushed herself to her feet and walked back inside the townhouse.

She stood in the kitchen, straining to listen. But she couldn't hear any evidence that the child was still crying. Satisfied that he must have fallen asleep, she poked in the fridge to figure out what they'd have for dinner.

The salad from the night before was still inside, so all she needed was a main dish. Something that Sebastian would like.

A peace offering.

He'd been excited to have the hamburgers Devon was going to make the night before, so she decided to go with something simple. She pulled out the ground beef, and then headed outside to start the grill.

It wasn't easy, but she managed. She watched the flames for a long moment, steeling herself to go in to confront Sebastian.

Back inside, she made her way down the hall to his room, which happened to be adjacent to hers. She opened the door, expected to find him cuddled up on his bed with his stuffed angel.

But he wasn't in the bed.

With a frown, she registered the fact that the stuffed angel wasn't there, either, which meant he must have taken it with him. To her room? She quickly went over to check.

When she didn't find him in her room, she went back into his bedroom. This time she searched everywhere, beneath the bed, in the closet, anywhere a small child could hide.

But she didn't find Sebastian, anywhere.

Panic swelled in her chest, but she tried to remain calm. He was only four and a half, he couldn't have gotten very far.

She spun on her heel and went back to the front door, mentally kicking herself for not locking it after Mrs. Alice had left.

A chill snaked down her spine when she noticed the heavy inside door had been left open. She jerked it out of her way, and burst through the second screen door, and out onto the porch.

"Sebastian? Sebastian!" Janelle didn't hesitate but ran out to the street, half expecting to see the little boy walking along the side of the road with his stuffed angel tucked beneath his arm.

Surely he couldn't have gone far?

But when she didn't see any sign of him, the panic she'd tried so hard to hold at bay erupted into a full-fledged attack.

"Sebastian!" she screamed at the top of her lungs. Rose's diner wasn't far, so she sprinted in that direction, telling herself she'd find Sebastian inside, enjoying a cup of hot chocolate. Right now, Josie was probably trying to call her to let her know Sebastian was there.

But when she barged into the diner, there was no sign of Sebastian's blond head.

"Janelle, honey, what's wrong?" Josie demanded, planting her hands on her ample hips.

"Have you seen Sebastian?" Her heart was pounding so loud she could barely hear herself speak. "Did he come up here to see you?"

"No, I haven't seen him. Why, is he missing?"

Tears welled in her eyes, blurring her vision. "Yes," she choked. "I can't find him. I—I think he ran away."

"Listen, go back home," Josie told her in a no-nonsense tone. "I'll call the sheriff's department."

Janelle nodded, and swiftly turned to head back outside. She broke into a run, trying to get back home in case Sebastian was actually there, waiting for her.

Maybe he'd been hiding somewhere else in the townhouse. But where? The place wasn't all that big.

Then she remembered the empty side of the townhouse. Had he found a way to get inside? Was it possible that Zack Crain hadn't locked up the night after the robbery?

She checked the front door, but it was locked. She ran around to the lake side and pulled on the patio doors.

They were locked too.

Without wasting a second, she hurried inside her own townhouse, this time checking each room systematically, looking anywhere a small child may try to hide.

But a few minutes later, she knew there was no escaping the truth.

Sebastian was gone.

She'd lost her sister's son.

10

D evon tapped his fingers on the desk, waiting for Zack Crain to answer his cell phone. He wanted the fingerprint results and couldn't understand why Zack hadn't kept him in the loop. Surely, they were back by now?

"Crain," Zack's clipped voice carried across the line.

"It's Dev. I hear you have the fingerprint results from the break-in at Janelle's place."

There was a small pause before Zack responded. "Yeah, I just got them about an hour ago. I needed to check a few things out before breaking the news to Janelle."

A wave of apprehension made Dev grip the phone tightly. "What news?"

He could hear Zack's sigh. "Does the name Grant Gardner mean anything to you?"

"Janelle mentioned that Sebastian's father's name was Grant, but I have no clue what his last name is. And he's supposed to be in jail."

"Yeah, well the finger prints in her house belong to

Grant Gardner and he just happens to have been released from jail, three days before the break-in."

He swallowed hard. "That's no coincidence."

"I don't think so either," Zack admitted. "And it's pretty interesting that he found her so quick. Not only that, but I showed his mug shot to Gretchen and she positively identified him, too. We have him on the burglary, if we can find him."

Dev stood and headed out to his squad. "I'm going over to talk to Janelle. Any chance you can find out if this Grant dude is driving a silver sedan?"

"I can try, but why? What makes you think he's driving a silver car?"

He resisted the urge to smack himself upside the head. He should have gone with his instincts. He knew that silver car parked near Janelle's was a sign of trouble. "I've seen a silver car hanging around outside the townhouse."

"That jerk," Zack muttered harshly.

Yeah, his feelings exactly. "Anything else? Do we know where Grant might be staying?"

"The Crystal Lake motel isn't far from Janelle's, I'll try there first." Zack hesitated, then added, "The guy has a history of domestic violence. Do you think he's going to try and hurt her?"

"I don't know," Dev forced himself to answer honestly. "But I'm not going to wait to find out. Call me if you find him at the motel, okay?"

"Sure thing."

Dev disconnected from the call and almost immediately another call came in, this time it was Janelle. He didn't want to believe that Josie could have gotten the scoop already, but crazier things had happened. "Hi Janelle," he greeted her cheerfully.

"Dev? Sebastian's gone. I need your help to find him!" The hysteria in her voice caused his gut to clench with fear.

"What do you mean, gone?" He jammed the key into the ignition and quickly started the engine. He figured he could be at Janelle's place in ten minutes flat if he used lights and sirens.

"He's gone, I left him alone in his room after his temper tantrum and now he's gone! I—I think he ran away from home. I need you and the other deputies to help me find him."

The timing of the boy's disappearance bothered him. "I'm on my way," he promised. "But Janelle, listen to me. Have you seen the silver car lately?"

"No, why?" she asked with a sniff.

The image of her crying was like a kick to the chest, but there was no time to. "We know the identity of the burglar, Grant Gardner, Sebastian's father. We matched his fingerprints. And Gretchen identified him, too."

"Grant?" There was a flash of anger in her tone. "You think Grant is here in Crystal Lake?"

"Yeah, we do. Just hang tight, I'm on my way."

"Hurry," she begged, before disconnecting from the line.

He punched the gas and took the turns that lead to Janelle's townhouse as fast and safely as possible. He couldn't believe that Sebastian was missing. Janelle had every right to be frantic.

The thought of the little boy in the hands of his father made Dev's blood run cold. Did Grant understand Sebastian's medical needs? Did the guy realize the child needed peritoneal dialysis exchanges to stay healthy? And what on earth possessed the guy to try and play father to Sebastian now?

Dozens of possibilities flashed through his mind, but at

the end of the day, Dev didn't think Grant really wanted custody of Sebastian. With his history of being an IV drug user, he was very much afraid the guy had something else on his mind.

Like kidnapping for ransom.

JANELLE PACED the sidewalk in front of the townhouse, trying to formulate some sort of plan as to where Sebastian might have gone. Was it possible Grant had something to do with his disappearance? She'd initially feared the little boy had decided to run away, especially after their fight over Mrs. Alice, but that was before Devon had told her that Sebastian's father's fingerprints had been found inside her house.

Grant had broken into her house. Had stolen her television and her computer. Pawned Lisa's ruby ring.

For money? Highly likely. It wouldn't be the first time Grant had robbed the people closest to him.

Hard to believe the authorities actually let Grant out of jail, but obviously everything she'd read about the problems with overcrowding within the prison system was true.

She heard police sirens long before she caught sight of Devon's squad car blazing up the road, red and blue lights flashing. He was barely out of the vehicle when she launched herself at him.

"We have to find Sebastian!"

"I know, we will." His strong arms held her close and she tried to calm her racing heart by filling her head with his familiar scent.

But even having Devon there wasn't enough to soothe her ragged nerves. She pulled out of his embrace, staring up at him intently. "How will we find him? Are you sending out search parties? What can I do to help?"

"First I need you to tell me exactly what happened," Dev said. "When was the last time you saw Sebastian?"

She swallowed a wave of frustration. Talking was not high on her agenda right now; she wanted, needed to *do* something. But she forced herself to think through the last few hours and tell Devon what she remembered.

"Mrs. Alice came to watch Sebastian's exchange around 12:30 in the afternoon. She left shortly afterwards, maybe close to 2:00 or so. Sebastian had a bit of a temper tantrum, so I sent him to his room." Her throat closed and her eyes welled with tears. She knew that Sebastian's disappearance was all her fault. She'd handled things badly and now the little boy was gone.

As if he could read her mind, Dev put a hand on her shoulder. "You did what hundreds of parents do when their kids throw a tantrum. Being sent to his room isn't anything to feel bad about."

She swiped at her eyes and shook her head. "It's worse," she said hoarsely. "I could still hear him screaming so I went outside to sit down by the lake."

"Don't, Janelle," Dev said softly. "Don't beat yourself up over this. You didn't do anything wrong."

"Then why is Sebastian missing?" she asked sharply. "Of course I was wrong! If I hadn't left the house he'd still be here."

"Stop it," Dev's tone was firm. "Blaming yourself isn't going to help. I need you to focus, okay? How long were you outside?"

He was right, she knew logically he was right. But that fact didn't make her feel any better. She took a deep breath and thought back. "Fifteen minutes, maybe twenty. I went back inside the house and went to listen by his door. I didn't open it, because I thought he might have cried himself to sleep. I started dinner, and then went to wake him up. But he was gone." The image of his rumpled, yet achingly empty bed was firmly etched in her mind.

"Okay, so Sebastian was in his room for less than an hour all told, right?"

An hour didn't seem long, but in reality it was an eternity. "Yes," she whispered. "Forty-five minutes, an hour at the most."

"So then what?" Devon prompted.

"I thought he'd run away, so I ran outside calling his name. He wasn't anywhere along the road, and I thought he might have made his way down to Rose's café, so I went there. But Josie hadn't seen him." The hysteria building inside threatened to explode.

Sebastian!

Devon lightly clasped her shoulders, forcing her to meet his gaze. "Don't panic, there's still plenty of light. We'll find him, okay?"

She wanted to believe that, and forced herself to nod.

"Let's go inside for a minute, I want to be sure there wasn't a note left behind."

A note? "Sebastian can't write," she protested, as they walked up to the front door.

"A note from Grant," Dev clarified.

"I searched the house for Sebastian, under his bed, in the closet, anywhere he might think of to hide," she protested. But she followed him inside, hoping she'd missed something.

Rushing down the hall, she flung open his bedroom door and stood on the threshold, peering around the room as if a note might have materialized in her absence.

But there was no note. Nothing of any sort left behind that she could see.

Janelle put a hand to her chest, fighting to breathe normally. Devon was right, self-recriminations and panic weren't going to help find Sebastian.

"What's this?" Devon asked, walking toward one of the bedroom windows.

She blinked, surprised that there was in fact the edge of a piece of white lined paper taped to the outside of the window, near the window frame. When the spring breeze blew past, the edge of the paper lifted up and away from the window, making it difficult to see.

Before she could move, Devon had brushed past her to head back outside. She followed in his wake, hope blooming in her chest. The note was a positive sign, right? This could be a clue that Devon and the other officers could use to help them find Sebastian.

Dev stood outside her son's bedroom window, reading the note. When he reached up to take it, he lightly caught her wrist, preventing her from touching it. "We need to check for fingerprints, Janelle."

She couldn't suppress a groan of frustration. "But that will take days, Devon." They didn't have days. They didn't even have hours.

There was no telling what might happen if Sebastian didn't get his next peritoneal dialysis treatment.

"Janelle?" Dev's voice broke through her torturous thoughts. "Does this look like Grant's handwriting to you?"

She stared at the note that appeared to be written in haste. *I have Sebastian. It will cost you ten grand to get him back.* There was a phone number with a Milwaukee area code scribbled along the bottom.

"It could be," she said. "But to be honest I only glanced at the letters he sent my sister from prison, begging her to give him a second chance."

"Do you still have those letters?"

Tears threatened again as she shook her head. "No, I didn't keep them. He physically abused Lisa, especially when he was under the influence, and to be honest, I didn't want him to have contact with Sebastian. I was afraid he'd do something drastic. And now-he has."

"It's okay, we can still compare his writing to court documents he would have needed to sign. But at this point, I think we can rule out the possibility of Sebastian running away on his own. It could be that Grant was hanging around and happened to hear the argument. Maybe he even used bits of the fight to get Sebastian to come along with him."

She could easily see how that could have worked, despite the fact that Grant was virtually a stranger to the boy. Grant was still Sebastian's biological father regardless of the fact the courts had severed his custody rights secondary to the abuse. She tried to think back. "Sebastian was wearing blue jeans and a red t-shirt with a dinosaur on the front. He also took his stuffed angel with him."

"Stuffed angel?" Dev looked confused.

She sniffled and swiped at her face. "When I first brought Sebastian home with me, he kept asking about when his mommy was coming home. I told him she was in heaven, but he couldn't grasp the concept. So I bought him a stuffed angel and told him that his mommy was up in heaven with God but that she sent the angel for him to hug and to hold at night when he was afraid."

This time when Dev reached out for her, she collapsed against him, pressing her face into the hollow of his shoulder.

"I can't lose him, Dev, I just can't," she whispered.

"You won't. I promise I'll do everything in my power to find him."

She nodded, knowing that Devon was a good cop, all of the Hope County Sheriff's deputies were good cops. But the relentless fear continued to gnaw at her. "Will you pray with me?"

"Of course I will." Devon pulled her hands up to the center of his chest and held them there. He bowed his head. "Dear Lord, we ask You to please keep Sebastian safe and healthy in Your care. Please grant us the wisdom and guidance to find him, so we can bring him home, Amen."

"Amen," she responded. Lifting her head she gazed up at him. "Thanks, Dev."

"You're welcome." Another cop car pulled up in front of her house and Janelle was relieved to see two more deputies making their way toward them.

She recognized Ian Kramer and Zack Crain. "Have you found something?" Zack called.

"A note taped to the outside of the kid's window." Devon gestured toward it. "I think we have to assume this is a kidnapping."

"Ten grand?" Ian echoed with a frown. "This dude isn't asking for a million dollars, so that means he knows Janelle wouldn't have that much."

She didn't bother to point out that she didn't have the ten grand, either. "We think Sebastian's father, Grant Gardner, took Sebastian. Grant is a known IV drug user, and he was hooked on Heroin before he was arrested for beating and robbing my sister three years ago."

The deputies exchanged serious looks. "Okay, and we think the suspect might be driving a silver sedan?"

"Yes, that's our theory," Devon replied. "There's a phone number on the note. I'm guessing he didn't have Janelle's cell number. I'll give him a call."

Janelle reached out to stop him. "Wait, I think I should

be the one to make the call. He doesn't need to know I've involved the police, does he? He might open up more to me."

Devon scowled, but reluctantly nodded. "Okay, you call, but let's go inside, I want you to put him on speaker, and we can't have any background noise."

Thankful for something to do, she waited while Devon took down the phone number from the note, leaving it right where they'd found it, and then headed back inside.

"Okay, here's how this works," Devon said as she pulled out a pen and paper. "You're going to ask for proof that he has Sebastian, insist on talking to him, okay? Then we'll take notes on what he says."

"What if he wants me to meet him with the money?" she asked.

"Go ahead and agree to make the arrangements. If he's using again, there's a good chance he'll make a mistake." Devon stared at her intently "Any questions?"

Too many to voice so she simply shook her head. The deputies crowded all around her in the kitchen, watching as she punched in the numbers and then set the phone in the center of the table. She waited with her pen poised above the paper.

The phone rang several times before going straight to voice mail. She took a deep breath and then spoke into the phone. "This is Janelle, I found your note and I have the money you requested. Please call me back at this number..." she said each number slowly, as if speaking to a child. "Please, I need to know Sebastian is all right."

She disconnected from the call and slumped in her chair. "I can't believe he didn't answer." She resisted the urge to throw the cell phone across the room.

"He'll call back," Devon assured her. "In the meantime, we'll try to figure out where he might be holding Sebastian."

She dropped her head into her hands, and did her best to put her faith and trust in God.

And Devon.

She had to believe that they'd find Sebastian, before it was too late.

11

Devon crossed over to where Zack and Ian, the other deputies, were standing off to the side in Janelle's kitchen. "Did either of you check the Crystal Lake Motel?"

"I did," Zack confirmed. "I flashed Grant's mug shot, no one remembers seeing him and there was no one registered under his name."

Dev had figured as much, but they needed to cover all bases. "What about the campground located down the highway?"

"I drove through it on my way here," Ian spoke up. "No sign of a silver car, but I didn't check every single camper."

"We need a game plan, and we can't wait forever for this guy to return Janelle's call. We need to spread out, try to figure out where he's hiding with Sebastian."

The other deputies nodded in agreement. "I'll head back to the campground," Ian volunteered.

"I'll flash Grant's photo up and down Main Street, see if anyone else recognizes him," Zack added.

"I'll drive around the lake," Dev decided. He turned back

toward Janelle, hating the thought of leaving her here alone. "We're going to start searching the area," he told her. "You have my cell number, right?" When she nodded, he continued, "I need you to call me the minute you hear from this guy. Don't try to do this alone, okay?"

"I won't," she promised, glancing toward the door as the other deputies left. "But isn't there something I can do, too? Sitting here doing nothing will drive me crazy."

He hesitated then nodded, realizing there was no reason she had to be here to get Grant's call since she'd left her cell number. In fact, it would save time if they were together. "Okay, you can ride along with me, an extra pair of eyes couldn't hurt."

"Thank you," she murmured.

He led the way outside, but then she stopped him with a hand on his arm. "Wait, let me get Sebastian's dialysis supplies so that I have them when we find him, just in case this takes longer than we expect."

"Sounds good." He was glad Janelle was maintaining a positive attitude about the outcome of the search. Logically he knew Grant had no reason to hurt the boy, but that didn't mean the guy would take good care of him, either. In fact, there was no telling what Grant might do, especially if he's under the influence.

Or worse, going through withdrawal. Was that why he hadn't answered Janelle's call? Maybe he wasn't capable of having a conversation? And if so, what was Sebastian doing? The poor kid would be scared out of his mind.

He slammed the door on that train of thought, knowing that it wouldn't help to think of the worst case scenario. Grant would call Janelle back. He'd give instructions on where they could meet in order to exchange the cash for the boy.

They'd get Sebastian back safe and sound.

When Janelle returned carrying the familiar backpack bulging with supplies, he opened the passenger door for her. "First thing we need to do is to stop at the bank."

"The bank?" she echoed, staring up at him in confusion. Then realization seemed to sink in. "Dev, I don't have ten thousand dollars. I barely have two thousand left in my savings account, I've been living off that money for the past few weeks."

"I know, but we need some cash to make it look good and we have to get it now, since the bank closes in less than an hour. I'll front the money, no problem." He closed the car door and jogged around to slide in behind the wheel.

"I can't let you do that," she said as he backed out of her driveway. "I'll use my money. Maybe if we get small bills it will look like I have the entire amount."

He wanted to argue, but held his tongue. In the end it didn't matter how much cash she took with her, Grant wouldn't be in a position to argue for more, he'd likely take what he could get.

Although Dev was equally determined they wouldn't lose one dollar of Janelle's money. Grant had already taken enough from her, the television, the computer, the ring. Seemed impossible that he could have blown through all that cash in just a few days, although Dev knew that he probably hadn't gotten very much for any of the items in the first place. Drug addicts generally only looked as far ahead as their next fix.

The trip down Main Street to the Hope County Bank didn't take long. It took some fast talking on his part to convince the bank to hand over the cash, and it wasn't until the bank owner, Edward Finch got involved that they were able to obtain the cash they needed.

Devon hauled the bags of cash out to the car and carefully stored them in the trunk.

Minutes later they were back on the road. "Okay, we need to keep an eye out for any sign of the silver car, and any possible remote hiding spots where Grant could be holding Sebastian. Also, let me know if you see any places for sale, those could be potential hiding places."

"Understood," Janelle said, gripping the cell phone tightly. She plastered her face against the window, taking her job of searching for the silver car very seriously.

He drove slow, giving them both plenty of time to scan the area. On occasion a call would come through the radio, making Janelle jump.

"The bartender at Pete's Pub recognized Gardner, but can't validate that he was driving a silver vehicle," Zack reported. "Last seen two nights ago."

"Ten-four," Dev responded, glancing over at Janelle who was obviously listening intently. "I'm approaching the north side of the lake."

"Campground all clear," Ian said a few minutes later. "No one claims to have recognized our guy, but I have my suspicions related to a couple of guys who I believe may have seen him. I found a small amount of dope in their camper, so I'm hauling them in to headquarters to book them for possession."

"Try to pressure them for the truth," Dev said. "Offer a lighter sentence and fine, if necessary."

"Ten-four," Ian responded.

"Do you think those guys sold Grant drugs?" Janelle asked, a small frown puckering her brow.

He gave her a grim nod. "Yeah, that's what Ian was insinuating. Hopefully Ian will convince them it's in their best interest to cooperate."

"Maybe we should check out the area closer to the campground?" she suggested, a flash of hope brightening her blue eyes.

"After we circle the lake," he agreed. "One step at a time."

She let out a heavy sigh and turned back to peer out the window. She understood that it wasn't easy to have patience, especially when a young child with medical needs was missing. But if Grant really had a car, then he could literally be anywhere.

Even someplace outside of Hope County.

Dev didn't want to think along those lines, at least not yet. He was determined to be thorough in their investigation, which meant checking the surrounding areas first. Besides, Grant would want to be close enough to Crystal Lake in order to make the exchange to get his money.

As Devon continued to drive, he found himself silently praying. Please, Lord, guide us to Sebastian! Keep this little boy safe in Your care, Amen.

JANELLE TRIED to focus her energy on finding the silver car, or any properties that were listed for sale, even though she kept remembering the argument that she'd had with Sebastian.

Ruminating over what she could have done differently wouldn't help. She needed to work with the Hope County Sheriff's Deputies to find her son.

It seemed that there were hardly any cars out on the road, and certainly no silver ones. Which was odd, since silver was a popular color.

She caught a glimpse of a small hand-made sign that

read *For Sale By Owner*, stuck in the ground near a tree-lined driveway on the north side of the road, across from the lake.

"Look, there's a for sale sign," she said excitedly, reaching over to grasp Devon's arm. "We should check it out."

"Good eye," Dev said, making an abrupt right hand turn onto the property. The squad car bumped over the uneven gravel driveway, as they approached the small cabin.

Janelle searched for any sign of life within the building, but the place appeared to be deserted. When she reached for the door handle, Dev stopped her.

"No, you need to wait here. Let me take a look around, first."

"Alright," she reluctantly agreed. She understood Devon's rationale, but that didn't make sitting there while he examined the place any easier.

But it was better than being stuck at home. She kept her eyes peeled on the building, hoping, praying she'd see Sebastian's face in a window.

Devon took his time, walking around the small cabin first, before making his way up to the front door. He knocked, but no one answered.

She held her breath, thinking he might break the door down, but instead he appeared to be speaking through his radio. She wished she could hear the conversation.

Minutes passed with agonizing slowness, and when he walked back toward the car, she wanted to scream in protest.

"Aren't we going to look inside?" she demanded, when he slid in behind the wheel. "Sebastian could be in there right now!"

"Calm down, Janelle. There's no evidence that anyone has been here in the past week, because it hasn't rained and there's a film of dirt on the front porch. There aren't any footprints other than my own."

His explanation caused her shoulders to slump. "Really?"

"Zack is running down the owner now, to see if we can get inside. But I wouldn't hold out any false hopes. I think if Grant and Sebastian had been here, we'd see some indication of that. I can't imagine Grant is that good at covering his tracks."

"So now what?" she asked, trying to hide the depths of her despair.

"We keep looking," Dev said calmly. "Are you still game? Or do you want me to take you back home?"

"I'm sticking with you."

"Good. Let's go." Dev executed a three point-turn so he could head back down the driveway toward the road.

They made a slow circle around the lake, ending up back on Main Street. Janelle couldn't help being discouraged by their lack of progress, especially when Dev returned to her townhouse.

A tiny flicker of hope in her heart convinced her Sebastian may have returned in her absence, but when she rushed back inside, she found the townhouse as empty as they had left it.

"What's next?" she asked, turning to face Devon.

"Zack is getting ready to send me a list of properties that are for sale in the area," he said, glancing down at his smart phone.

More properties? They hadn't found anything encouraging at the last few they'd looked at. She tried not to sound as tense and irritable as she felt. "Isn't there something else we can do?"

Dev didn't take umbrage with her tone. "Listen, we know

that Grant likely purchased drugs at the campsite. What if he took a tent and pitched it on some property that happens to be for sale? If it's a big enough lot, with trees for cover, no one would see them."

"That sounds like a possibility," she admitted, feeling better at his logic.

Devon's cell phone rang, and he quickly answered it. "Armbruster," he said in a formal tone.

She fell silent, able to hear a bit of the other person's conversation. "Confirmed drug buy."

"Good to know, what else did they have to say?" Devon asked.

She realized the campers must have admitted to selling drugs to Grant. The thought of him using again made her feel sick to her stomach. Especially since he had Sebastian with him.

Lost in her thoughts, she missed what the other deputy said. "Okay, thanks, Ian. It's good to know that we're on the right track. I'm waiting for a list of properties from Zack, once I get them we can split them up."

"What kind of drugs did Grant buy?" she asked when Dev disconnected from the call.

He grimaced. "Heroin," he admitted. "But again, the last time they saw Gardner was two days ago, the same night as the bartender. And one of the campers happened to be the one who sold Lisa's ring to Gretchen. We have a good connection and theory here, but we still haven't found anyone who has seen him in the last forty-eight hours."

Forty-eight hours to create a plan to kidnap Sebastian.

A lifetime.

She drew in a choppy breath. "It's past dinnertime," she said in a low tone. "I'm sure Sebastian is hungry."

"Don't, Janelle," Devon murmured. He stepped closer

and put his arm around her shoulders. "Don't think the worst. For all we know, Grant has food tucked away, especially if he's been camping up here."

She nodded and rested against him, trying to absorb some of his strength. "Why hasn't Grant called me back?" she asked, her voice rising in helpless frustration. "What's taking him so long?"

"I don't know," Devon admitted. "Maybe he's waiting for darkness to fall. Or maybe he thinks that the longer he waits, the more frantic you'll be to pay the money. There's just no telling what's going through his mind."

"He's on drugs, which means he might not be thinking clearly at all." She shivered and burrowed closer to Devon's warmth. "For all we know he could be passed out, leaving Sebastian unattended. That poor little boy is probably scared to death, wondering what will happen to him."

"Janelle, please," he begged, reaching down to lift her chin, forcing her to meet his gaze. "Please stop thinking like that. Fear will only paralyze us. We need to remember that Sebastian is smart. He'll manage just fine."

She really, really wanted to believe that. She forced a lop-sided smile. "Okay, you're right. Thank you, Devon. I couldn't handle this without you."

He stared down at her with fathomless deep brown eyes, and she almost thought he was going to kiss her, but the moment was broken when his phone chimed with an incoming message.

"This might be Zack's list," he said, releasing his hold on her.

She stepped back and rubbed her hands over her arms. What was wrong with her? She shouldn't have been thinking of kissing Devon. Not when Sebastian was out there, alone and afraid.

"Ian? It's Dev, I have the list of properties and am sending it to you, now." There was a moment of silence as Dev hit the message on his phone. Then he said, "I'll start at the top, you start at the bottom and we'll meet in the middle, okay?"

Janelle grabbed a jacket then decided to gather more things for Sebastian, in case they found him. She tossed his coat over her arm, and then went into the kitchen to pull out a box of cheesy fish crackers.

"I'm ready to go," she announced.

"Great." Devon glanced down at his list, then led the way outside to the car. "The first property isn't that far from the cabin that was listed for sale, we'll start there."

She nodded, grateful for something constructive to do. Although she couldn't help thinking that time was not on their side. Her phone hadn't rung even once, and her nerves were stretched thin with fear and worry. Yet as Dev drove, she continued to search for any sign of a silver car.

"What else did Ian have to say?" she asked. "You mentioned something about how it was good we're on the right track."

"The campers claimed Grant was driving a silver car, and that he had a tent, along with other camping gear."

She sucked in a quick breath. "So he was watching me for the past few days."

"Yeah." Devon's expression turned dark. "I wish I gotten his plate numbers long before this."

"No sense in looking back," she reminded him. "I've been doing that enough for the both of us."

He glanced at her with a wry grin. "Yeah, easier said than done, isn't it?"

"You got that right. I keep wishing I would have handled Sebastian's anger differently."

He tilted his head to the side. "You never mentioned what caused Sebastian's temper tantrum in the first place."

She swallowed hard then decided it was better to be honest. "You."

Dev did a double take. "What do you mean? What about me?"

"Remember how I found that retired nurse to babysit Sebastian?" When he nodded, she continued, "Well he didn't like her. He kept telling me that he only wanted you to babysit him. And when I told him that wasn't possible, he lost it." The argument seemed so petty now that Sebastian was gone.

Devon was silent for a long moment. "I'm sorry. I had no idea."

"It's not your fault. Sebastian has never had a father figure. Grant went to jail when he was barely a year old." She sighed, and then added, "To be honest, I didn't much like Mrs. Alice, either. She was old and crabby and as Sebastian put it, she smelled funny."

Devon's lips twitched with repressed humor. "So I should forgo showering the next time I visit you both?"

She managed a small smile. "I don't think that will help, Sebastian will still love you anyway. Ms. Alice smelled like moth balls."

The shrill ringing of her cell phone interrupted them. Her heart pounded in her chest as she glanced down at the screen, recognizing Grant's number.

"Hello?"

"I have—the boy," Grant's voice was slurred. "Got money?"

"Yes, I have the money," she said, speaking slowly and clearly so that he could understand her, despite whatever drugs he'd taken. "I'll pay you to get Sebastian back. Where can I meet you?"

"The woods…" his voice trailed off the rest of his speech garbled to the point she couldn't figure out what he was saying.

"Where in the woods? Tell me where to meet you?"

Seconds passed and then the line abruptly disconnected. She stared at the device and quickly pushed the redial button.

But Grant didn't answer, neither did Sebastian.

And she still had no idea where they were hiding.

12

D evon hated hearing the panic in Janelle's tone. "I can't believe it! Grant didn't tell me where to meet him!"

Devon understood her angst, but couldn't think of anything to say that would make her feel any better. He struggled to remain calm. "Take a breath and tell me exactly what he said."

"He said he had Sebastian and asked if I had the money, but he was clearly under the influence. When I asked where to meet him, he simply said, the woods, and then his voice trailed off. Now he's not answering the phone!" She thumped her fist on the phone as if that would help.

Devon tightened his grip on the steering wheel, battling a wave of frustration. Janelle had every right to be upset, but she needed him to be strong, so he did his best to maintain his professionalism.

"I grew up here, Janelle. I know these woods and so do the other deputies. We'll find him," he said, knowing that the mantra was likely getting old.

But he needed to believe it just as badly as she did. Despite the fact that Sebastian originally reminded him of what he'd loved and lost, he cared very much about the little guy.

The sun was dipping down on the horizon and he knew that it would be dark soon, making the task of finding Sebastian difficult, especially if they were hiding in the woods.

The wooded area along the north side of the lake covered a good twenty-thirty acres and since it wasn't damaged by the fire, the evergreen trees were thick and dense. The only good news was that the rest of the trees only had early spring buds on them, which might make it easier to find a tent.

Who was he kidding? Finding a tent in thirty acres would be nearly impossible. Especially since Sebastian's exchange was due soon.

In less than an hour.

So they had to try. Using his radio, he updated the rest of the deputies, asking them to meet him at the corner of Lake Drive and Elmhurst. From there, they'd have to formulate some sort of search plan.

But hiking through the woods at night wouldn't be easy. He radioed into the dispatch office. "Ask Sheriff Torretti if he'll call in a K9 search and rescue unit."

"Ten-four," the dispatcher responded.

Maybe he should have requested this earlier. He'd thought for sure that Grant would return Janelle's call to set up a meeting. But once they discovered how Grant had bought drugs from the other campers, he should have altered their game plan.

He'd made the wrong call, and both Janelle and Sebastian would pay the ultimate price for his mistake.

Dev did his best to shove his useless guilt aside. Focus. He needed to focus on saving Sebastian.

The meeting point was up ahead and he was glad to see that Ian was already there, waiting for them.

Devon rolled down his window. "Do you have extra flashlights?"

"Yep. I'm ready when you are."

"Where's Zack?" Devon asked, as he pushed open his car door and climbed out of the vehicle.

"I think that's him now," Ian said, gesturing to the twin pair of headlights approaching from the east.

Dev blew out a heavy breath. "Okay, we need to figure out where this jerk is hiding with Sebastian. The only clue we have is that there's a possibility they're in the woods. Although it doesn't make a lot of sense that he'd arrange for a meeting there."

"Guy's a druggie, who knows what's going on in his head?" Ian muttered darkly.

Dev silently agreed. Addiction was a terrible thing. It took good people and twisted them into someone who would do anything to get what they needed. Obviously Gardner wasn't thinking logically or rationally.

So if he was a drug user and had kidnapped a child, what would he do? Where would he go?

His radio buzzed. "Sheriff approved the K9 unit, should be there within twenty minutes or so," the dispatcher informed him.

Twenty minutes was too long. Although he wasn't going to turn down the offer of help, either. Glancing at Janelle's pinched features, the phone she held so tightly in her hand, he knew he'd search all night if necessary.

"Ten-four." He turned his attention to the other two deputies. "Are there more deputies coming?"

Zack nodded. "I reached the two night shift deputies, they're coming in early to assist."

Five deputies to cover thirty acres. It could be worse, but he felt as if twenty deputies wouldn't be enough. "All right, let's split up the area evenly between the five of us and spread out. The K9 unit will be coming soon, too. Once the dog is able to pick up the child's scent, our search field will narrow considerably."

"I want to help search, too," Janelle said, coming up to stand beside him.

He shook his head regretfully. "I'm sorry, but you'll need to wait here for the K9 unit. You have Sebastian's coat, they'll need that for the dogs. And being in the woods at night is dangerous, I don't want you to get lost, or worse, run into a hungry bear."

She shivered and crossed her arms protectively across her chest. "You're making that up, aren't the bears still in hibernation?"

"I wouldn't count on it," Ian spoke up. "We've had decent weather for the past week; I suspect they're up and about by now."

She blanched. "What if Grant and Sebastian run into a bear?"

Dev wished he'd have kept his mouth shut about the wildlife. Bears weren't the only threat: game warden Reese Weber had found bobcat tracks recently, too. Thankfully the deer and other small game wouldn't pose much of a problem.

"I'm sure they'll be fine," Devon said reassuringly.

Zack spread out a map of the area on the hood of Ian's squad car and glanced at Devon. "Okay, how do you want to split this up?"

Devon stared at the map for a moment, then tapped the

area to the west. "I'll start here."

"Okay, I'll take this one," Ian put his finger on another part of the map.

Zack nodded in agreement. "I'll take this area." He scribbled their names on the map, so that when the other deputies arrived they wouldn't end up in the same place. "Janelle, you're going to be our point person, okay?" He handed her a radio. "When the K9 unit arrives, you let us know. And when the other deputies arrive you show them this map. We're counting on you."

Janelle clipped the radio to the edge of her sweatshirt. "Okay. I can do this."

Dev was proud of the way she set her fear and panic aside to assist in any way possible. He wanted to pull her close and kiss her, but managed to hold back sensitive to the fact they weren't alone.

He lifted the heavy flashlight and headed into the woods on foot. As he made his way through the trees, listening intently for any human sounds, he abruptly remembered the shallow cave where he and Steven had played as kids.

The cave was little more than a crevasse in the side of a large hill, too shallow for a bear to consider using it as a place to hibernate. Not only was it a perfect hiding spot for a human, but it also happened to be in his search area.

He decided to check there first, especially since the hill wasn't too far away. Using his compass he made his way in a north-east direction.

Slowly sweeping the flashlight from side to side, the beam cut through the darkness. In the daylight, he might be able to find Grant's tracks, but searching in the dark wouldn't be easy and he didn't want to waste precious time.

The radio remained silent as he made his way through the woods. Devon tried to walk fast without making too much noise, but the sound of a twig snapping beneath his heel echoed like a gunshot through the darkness.

It took longer than he anticipated to reach the crevasse in the hill. When he saw the area reflected in the beam of his flashlight, he aimed his light down on the ground, covered the lens with his hand to dim the light and slowed his pace, moving as quietly as possible.

He debated calling for Sebastian by name, unwilling to alert Grant to his presence if indeed they were tucked away in there. He edged closer and strained to listen.

His high hopes deflated when he couldn't hear anything but silence.

Just as he was about to give up, he heard a weird scratching noise.

Something was inside the crevasse, but was it animal?

Or human?

JANELLE SILENTLY PRAYED over and over again as she waited from inside Devon's squad car for news. Any news. Being here alone wasn't nearly as frightening as wondering what was going on in the woods.

Sebastian was well overdue for his peritoneal dialysis exchange. Would he be feeling sick as a result? Or just tired? She had been meticulous about doing his exchanges so she had no idea what to expect him to feel like when he missed one.

Deep down, she hoped he was asleep, dreaming of good things rather than being huddled someplace, alone and afraid.

She took a small measure of comfort in knowing that he had his stuffed angel with him. And of course, she firmly believed God was watching over him.

What was taking them so long? She stared blindly through the windshield, the darkness so complete that she couldn't see more than a few feet in any direction.

Headlights shimmered on the horizon and she couldn't deny feeling relieved that more deputies were on their way to help search. She was so afraid they'd decide to hold off and wait until morning.

When the car pulled up and parked alongside the others, she slid out of the car to greet them, a bit surprised when she realized that Sheriff Luke Torretti was walking toward her.

"Hi Sheriff," she greeted him. "Devon asked me to stay here, to show you the map so you'd know where they're searching."

The Sheriff nodded and then reached out to take her chilly hand in his. "I'm sorry that you have to go through this, Janelle," he said in a low voice full of sympathy. "I want you to know we're doing everything in our power to find your son."

Tears threatened and she rapidly blinked them away. "Thank you. Is the K9 unit here? I have Sebastian's jacket."

"Right here, Ma'am," a deep voice said from behind the sheriff. A tall man with jet black hair stepped forward, a large yellow Lab at his side. "I'm Seth Bertram and this is my dog, Buck. Will you hand me the boy's jacket?"

Janelle was impressed at how well behaved Buck was. He sat motionless beside his master. Seth took the jacket and then held it for Buck to sniff.

The dog buried his nose in the fabric for several long moments before Seth straightened. "I'll keep the jacket with me, if you don't mind," he said.

"Of course I don't mind. Thanks for your help."

"It's no problem, Ma'am. This is what we've trained for."

Seth turned toward the Sheriff. "We'll start out by walking back and forth to see if Buck picks up the scent."

"Sounds good." Sheriff Torretti turned to Janelle. "Any news yet?"

"Nothing." She couldn't begin to say how much the lack of information haunted her. She'd assumed there would be regular updates, but at this point, it was clear the deputies didn't have anything to report.

What if they were looking in the wrong place? She reviewed the brief, disjointed conversation she'd had with Grant. Technically, he hadn't said, "Meet us in the woods."

She reminded herself that they'd already searched all the other possible places: the vacant properties, the motel, the campground, and up and down Main Street. They hadn't checked the hiking trail along the lake, since the wildfire last fall had destroyed the area.

Where else could they be?

The woods made the most sense, but suddenly she was overwhelmed with doubt. Since when had Grant ever been logical?

Since never.

"Good boy," Seth's deep voice cut through the night.

Janelle rushed over. "Did you find something?"

Seth nodded. "Buck here picked up the boy's scent. Sheriff, do you want to come along?"

Sheriff Torretti nodded. "Yes. Janelle, stay here and let the others know the K9 dog picked up the boy's scent. We'll be in touch as soon as we have something."

She resisted the urge to beg him to stay. Better that Seth and Buck have all the help and support they need. She returned to the car, watching as the two men bearing flashlights followed the yellow lab's lead through the trees.

She did as she was told, using the radio to let all the

deputies know that the K9 unit was following Sebastian's scent. Both Zack and Ian responded affirmatively.

But she hadn't heard anything from Devon.

The bobbing of the Sheriff's and the K9 cop's flashlights grew dim, until the darkness swallowed them up. She bit her lip to keep from crying out in despair. Tilting her head back so she could gaze up at the stars hovering in the inky sky, she prayed once again.

Please keep Sebastian safe in Your care!

Minutes crawled by slowly, and the night air grew chilly, forcing her once again back inside Devon's squad car. His male, musky scent lingered inside, giving her a small measure of comfort.

When her radio crackled a few minutes later, she nearly jumped out of her skin. It took a minute for her to recognize Devon's voice. "Janelle? Do you copy?"

Eagerly she pressed the button. "Yes, Devon, I'm here. What happened? You didn't respond earlier, did you find something?"

"Yes. I have Sebastian, over."

She clenched her fingers on the radio with excitement. "You found him? Is he okay?"

"He's okay," there was a brief pause before he continued "I'm carrying him out now."

The hesitancy in his tone caused a frisson of worry to snake down her spine. Sebastian was just okay? What did that mean? Was the boy unconscious? Unable to talk?

Had going too long without his exchange caused some sort of harm? And if so, was it temporary?

Or permanent?

She leaped out of the front passenger seat to grab the backpack of supplies she brought from home out of the back. The minute Devon arrived with Sebastian, she intended to be ready.

Once she had everything ready to go, she turned and gazed toward the woods, trying to catch the glimmer of light that would indicate they were close. She desperately needed to see her son for herself, to touch him, to hold him.

But as she stood there, looking at nothing, she realized that Devon hadn't said anything about Grant. Because he was there but unconscious and unable to put up a fight?

Or because he'd disappeared, leaving Sebastian alone to die?

13

D evon carried Sebastian, the stuffed angel firmly wedged between them, his long strides eating up the ground as he made his way back toward the squad car where Janelle was waiting.

"Hang in there, Sebastian," he murmured, wrapping his coat more tightly around the child. The boy's hands had been like ice when he'd arrived, but they were beginning to warm up nicely.

"Okay," the child's voice was faint and he was so sleepy that Devon couldn't be sure that Gardner hadn't drugged him up to keep him quiet.

Not that the guy would be drugging anyone ever again. When Devon arrived, he'd found Grant dead of what Dev could only assume was an accidental drug overdose.

He felt sad that Grant had died so young, like so many others who ended up hooked on drugs. But thankfully, Sebastian hadn't seemed to notice the guy who'd taken him from Janelle was dead.

A light from the west grew brighter and soon Devon

realized that the K9 unit was coming toward him. "Armbruster?" a familiar voice called out. "Is that you?"

"Yes, Sheriff. I have Sebastian, but the guy who kidnapped him is dead."

"Dead, how?" Sheriff Torretti asked, frowning as he approached. "I don't recall hearing a gunshot."

"No sir, I didn't shoot him. He was crumpled up on the ground when I arrived with a syringe hanging out of his arm. I'm pretty sure it was an accidental overdose, but we'll need to notify the ME to verify that."

Sheriff Torretti blew out a heavy breath. "What a waste."

Devon silently agreed. He glanced at the K9 officer. "I'm Deputy Armbruster. I can take you back to where Grant's body is located as soon as I hand Sebastian over to Janelle. He was pretty cold when I found him."

"I'm Deputy Seth Bertram, and this is my partner, Buck. We can probably find the dead guy ourselves, Buck is pretty good at that kind of thing," Seth said. "No need to rush back."

Devon nodded. "Let me know if you can't find it for some reason." He edged past the two men, grateful when Sebastian squirmed a bit against him.

"Dev?" Sebastian asked in a whisper.

"Yeah, buddy, I'm here. You're safe now, nothing to worry about, okay?"

"'Kay," the boy mumbled.

Devon's heart squeezed in his chest as he pressed a kiss to the top of Sebastian's head. In the short time that he'd been around the child, he'd come to care about him, deeply.

He cared to the point where the thought of not seeing him, or Janelle again, was intolerable.

Yet could he really stay here in Crystal Lake for the rest of his life? Janelle made it clear she loved the small town, with its community atmosphere. And up until recently, he'd enjoyed it, too.

But what about his dream of making a difference, like his brother Steven had done? Was that God's plan for him?

Or had God's plan been about staying here to find Sebastian?

Dev knew there was time to think about the future, but right now, he needed to pick up the pace. Janelle would want to get started on Sebastian's dialysis exchange right away.

When he emerged from the woods, Janelle came running toward him, her eyes full of gratitude. "Oh, Devon, thank you for finding him. Thank you so much!"

"Let me carry him to the car," he said, when she reached up to take Sebastian. "He was chilled when I found him, so I've wrapped him up in my coat. We'll need to keep him as warm as possible."

"Okay." She kept her hand on the child's arm, as if she couldn't bear to be separated from him for another second. When they reached his squad car, he waited for her to open the back door before he crouched down and gently set the boy inside.

"Oh, Sebastian," Janelle murmured, kissing his cheek. "I'm so glad you're okay. Let's get this catheter connected to a drainage bag."

Dev stepped back, watching for a moment as Janelle washed her hands with sanitizer before moving Sebastian's clothing just enough to expose his catheter. It didn't take long to begin draining the fluid from his abdomen and she gently pulled the coat back around him for warmth.

"Mommy?" Sebastian asked, reaching his hand toward Janelle.

She leaned in and took his hand, pressing a kiss to his fingers. "Yes, Sebastian, I'm right here."

A faint smile crossed his features. "I wuv you."

"Oh sweetie, I love you, too." Janelle's voice broke and Devon quickly stepped forward to draw her into his embrace.

Janelle turned and wrapped her arms around his waist. "What happened to Grant?" she asked in soft voice, obviously not wanting Sebastian to overhear.

"He's dead, Janelle," Dev informed her. "Looks like he killed himself by overdosing on drugs."

She buried closer, tightening her grip on him. "That's so terrible," she whispered. "But I can't deny being glad he's no longer a threat to us. To Sebastian."

"I know, it's awful to lose someone so young, especially when he might have been able to turn his life around with treatment. But the important thing is, we have Sebastian back, unharmed. And I don't think Sebastian knows Grant's dead, either. He was pretty groggy when I found him."

That news caused her head to come up. "Groggy? Did Grant drug him?"

Dev hesitated and shrugged. "I honestly don't know. Sebastian was chilled when I found him, so it could be that he was a bit hypothermic, or exhausted, or even because he was late in getting his exchange."

She drew a deep breath. "Most likely, a combination of all three," she agreed. She stared up at him for a moment. "How did you find him so fast? The K9 unit had barely gotten started."

He flashed a wry grin. "I got lucky," he admitted. "I remembered how Steven and I played in this area when we were younger. We found this crevasse in the side of a hill, shallow enough to be safe from predators. I was so glad I managed to get there in time to get Sebastian out of the cold."

"Me, too." She levered up on her tiptoes to brush his cheek with her lips. "Words can't express how much I appreciate what you've done for me, Devon."

He longed to kiss her properly, but wasn't sure if she really felt the same way. Right now, she was simply grateful for having her son back, safe and sound.

For all he knew, she still only cared about him as a friend, while his feelings for her had somehow become much more complicated than that.

JANELLE GLANCED at the dashboard clock, wincing when she realized that the hour was approaching midnight. As much as she needed to get a paycheck, she couldn't go into work the next morning.

She was exhausted, as was Sebastian, but that wasn't the real reason. After everything that had transpired in the last few hours, there was no way she could bear to leave Sebastian with Mrs. Alice.

Yet she hated the thought of calling in to work, asking for yet another unpaid personal day. But what choice did she have? It was too late to find someone to switch shifts for her.

Devon pulled into her driveway and then shut off the car. "I'll carry Sebastian in for you," he offered.

Since she needed to haul in all the supplies, she nodded. "Okay, thanks."

They both climbed out of the car and she pulled the backpack up from between her knees and looped it over her shoulder. Sebastian had been so tired he'd barely eaten any of the fish crackers she'd brought along.

He was safe, and that was all that mattered, she reminded herself. No doubt, he'd wake up starving for breakfast.

She used her key to unlock the door and held it for Devon as he carried Sebastian inside. She flipped on the kitchen light, then went down the hall to help tuck Sebastian into bed.

"G'night, Dev. G'night, Mommy," Sebastian murmured before snuggling into the blankets she brought up beneath his chin.

That was the second time he'd called her *Mommy*, and as much as she rejoiced in the endearment, she knew that it was possible Sebastian was confused.

In the morning she'd be Nana again.

She leaned down to press a gentle kiss on his forehead before straightening up to ease out of the room. Devon waited at the doorway, a tender smile on his face.

"I'm glad he's doing all right," Devon whispered as she closed the bedroom door part way, leaving it open an inch in case Sebastian suffered from any nightmares as the night wore on.

"You and me, both," she agreed. As she headed for the kitchen, she pulled out her phone. "I need to call the hospital to let them know I won't be in tomorrow morning."

"I thought you had that woman all lined up to watch Sebastian?" Devon asked with a puzzled frown.

"I just can't do it," she confided. "Sebastian didn't like her and after everything he's been through, I can't just leave him with her in the morning. I'll have to try and find someone else to watch him."

"I'll come and stay until 2:30," Devon offered in a low husky voice.

She appreciated his generosity, but she couldn't just

leave work early, either. "No, that's not necessary. I'm lucky to get home by four in the afternoon, so we'd need someone to watch him for that period of time." It took her a minute to notice she'd used the pronoun *we*, as if they were really in this together.

But they weren't. A fact she needed to remember.

She cleared her throat, hoping Devon hadn't noticed her subconscious slip. "Don't worry, I'm sure I'll find someone to watch Sebastian. I can always offer to pick up some other shift." She frowned, wondering if Tina, the young woman who finished her certified nursing assistant training would get back to her soon enough to possibly pick up a shift over the weekend?

Devon didn't seem inclined to leave, but stood leaning against the kitchen counter while she called into work.

Thankfully, the charge nurse didn't seem too upset by the news. "We're actually staffed okay for the day shift tomorrow, Janelle," Kimberly said. "But we're short staffed this weekend, so let us know if you can help out at all."

She let out her breath in a relieved sigh. "I'm hoping to find someone to watch Sebastian over the weekend, so that is a definite possibility. I'll let you know for sure when I have someone lined up."

"Okay, sounds good," Kimberly said cheerfully.

Janelle disconnected from the call. Then she called Mrs. Alice, wincing at the late hour. Thankfully the woman didn't answer so she left a brief message, cancelling her for the next morning. Then she glanced at Devon who was staring at her intently.

"I'm off this weekend," he said in a casual tone. "I'd be happy to watch Sebastian."

She would have liked nothing better, but she shook her head. "I don't think that's a good idea," she protested.

His gaze darkened. "Why not?"

Her heart literally ached in her chest, but she knew she needed to stand firm "because Sebastian is already getting too attached to you, Devon."

"So? I'm pretty attached to him, too."

Was he being obtuse on purpose? "And what about when you move away for your new job?" she asked in a challenging tone. "I'll tell you what will happen you'll break his tiny heart into a zillion pieces."

He opened his mouth to protest, but then closed it again. He pushed himself upright and then walked past her toward the door.

She wanted to call out to him, to stop him from leaving, but at the same time, she wasn't about to prevent him from pursuing his future.

Too bad Devon didn't care about her in the same way she cared for him.

And when he left the townhouse, shutting the door quietly behind him, she collapsed into a chair and covered her face with her hands.

Sebastian was safe there was no reason to cry.

But she couldn't hold back the tears that trickled down her cheeks, anyway.

DEVON LEFT Janelle's townhouse feeling as if he'd been kicked in the gut.

When his cell phone rang, he answered it with a growl. "Armbruster."

"Hey Dev, I'd like your statement before you head home," Sheriff Torretti said in a tone that didn't leave room for argument. "We found Grant Gardner's body and are sending it to Dr. Hauf, the medical examiner."

Duty calls, he thought with a sigh. "Sure thing. I'll get right on that."

"By the way, Captain Mark Anderson from the Madison PD called asking me to give you a reference," the sheriff continued. "Of course I gave you high marks."

The news should have cheered him up, but it didn't. "Thank you, sir."

There was a brief pause, and Devon stood by his squad car, waiting for the sheriff to finish up the conversation. "I'm sorry to see you go, Armbruster. I'll miss having you on my team, you're a good cop."

Dev rubbed the back of his neck. "Thank you, sir. I want you to know that I've enjoyed working for you."

"Then why are you so anxious to leave?"

He repeated what he'd told Janelle just a few days ago. "I guess I feel like I should be making a bigger difference in people's lives. You're a good sheriff Hope County doesn't have a lot of crime."

"But we have some crime, and you might want to think about the fact that helping people you know on a first name basis can be more rewarding than helping strangers," Sheriff Torretti pointed out. "In fact, I'm not sure what would have happened to Sebastian if you hadn't known where to look for him."

He thought back to how chilled the boy was when he'd arrived. What if he'd been a few hours later? He didn't want to think about the fact that Sebastian may have died.

"Someone else may have thought of that hiding spot, too," he said breaking the silence.

"Not sure I agree with you on that. Zack grew up here, too, but he didn't know anything about that crevasse in the side of the hill. Frankly, I have no idea how Gardner managed to stumble upon it."

Dev was shocked to hear that Zack Crain didn't have any knowledge of that area of the woods. "Pure luck, probably," he said in response to the sheriff's comment about Gardner. "I'm on my way to headquarters now," he said, changing the subject as he slid behind the wheel. "You'll have my report tonight, sir."

Another slight pause, before the sheriff responded. "Thanks, Devon. You did a good job, tonight."

The sheriff disconnected from the call before he could respond, and Devon set his phone aside and turned the key in the ignition.

As he drove, he kept thinking about what Sheriff Torretti had said about helping people you know being more rewarding than helping total strangers.

Was he right about that? Hadn't Janelle mentioned something similar?

The thought nagged at him as he drove into the parking lot and trudged into the building. When he booted up his computer, he was surprised to see that he had a message from the Madison Police Department, asking him to call them as soon as possible if he was still interested in the position.

And he was interested, wasn't he?

He stared at the e-mail, belatedly realizing that he hadn't checked his computer prior to responding to Janelle's panicked phone call. Of course, it was too late to do anything about the message now. He'd have to remember to call first thing in the morning.

And do what? Agree to take the job if they offered it to him?

He couldn't believe he was having second thoughts about moving away from Crystal Lake. He'd sent out his resume months ago. He'd be foolish to turn down the opportunity.

But truthfully, he wasn't nearly as thrilled with the idea of moving any longer not since getting to know Janelle and Sebastian.

His heart clenched in his chest. He hadn't intended to fall in love ever again. So why was he picturing a future with Janelle and Sebastian?

Ignoring the message wasn't easy, but he needed to write up his report for the Sheriff. When something this big happened in their small county, he knew that there would be lots of scrutiny on how they'd handled the case.

Devon couldn't deny there were a few things he could have done differently.

But he didn't have many regrets, since he'd found a way to deliver on his promise to bring Sebastian home to Janelle.

And she'd turned around and refused his offer to watch Sebastian over the weekend while she went to work.

Maybe he was fooling himself, thinking that he had a reason to stay here in Crystal Lake.

He finished his report, printed it out and set a copy on the Sheriff's desk.

And as he drove home to his dark, empty house, he tried not to think about the fact that if he took the job in Madison, he'd just be trading one dark, empty, lonely house for another.

14

Janelle didn't sleep well that night, thanks in part to the way Devon had left so abruptly when she'd declined his offer to babysit over the weekend. In the early morning light, she found herself second-guessing her decision not to have Devon stay with Sebastian while she went to work.

She wanted to do the right thing for Sebastian. He was already emotionally attached to Devon, would one more weekend hurt? Even if Dev did get another job he'd have to give a two week notice to the Sheriff, wouldn't he?

The thought of not seeing Devon again after a few weeks, filled her with sorrow. Not just because she'd miss his friendship and support, which she would.

But she'd miss his hugs, and his kisses, even more.

She gave a little sigh, wishing she'd gotten rid of Lane long before Sebastian came into her life. Maybe she would have noticed Devon earlier, and gotten to know him better, before he'd made the decision to move on to a big city.

Although truthfully, she had no reason to believe Devon

felt remotely the same way about her. She knew from Josie just how much Devon had loved Debra, his fiancée.

"Mommy?" Sebastian's weak voice calling her from his bedroom interrupted her thoughts.

A warm glow settled in the region of her heart at the way he said *Mommy*, and she hoped he'd continue calling her that from now on. She hurried down the hall to his bedroom. "Good morning, sweetie, how are you feeling?"

"Hungry," he said rubbing his eyes with his chubby fists.

She lifted him up and gave him a hug and a kiss, which he returned enthusiastically, before carrying him into the living room. There was no reason he couldn't walk, but she wanted to keep him close after everything that had happened the night before. "What would you like for breakfast?" she asked as she placed him on the sofa.

"French toast, please." He gazed up at her, his wide blue eyes filled with hope. "Is Dev here, too?"

She was caught off guard by the question, why would he think Devon stayed here over night? Maybe Sebastian's memory was a bit fuzzy. "No, he went home last night after he rescued you." She hadn't asked Sebastian about what happened, figuring that he'd tell her when he was ready to talk. The last thing she wanted to do was to bring up bad memories. "Dev has to work again today, so I don't know if he'll have time to stop by."

Sebastian's expression reflected his disappointment. "Couldn't you call him?"

She hesitated, unsure of the right approach. Last night she'd wanted to protect Sebastian from getting even more attached to Devon than he was already. But was it better to wean him slowly over the next few days? Or cut the ties cold turkey?

Janelle knew that if she called Devon, he'd come to see

Sebastian, regardless of how they'd parted last night. He'd never let his anger keep him from seeing Sebastian.

Just one of the many reason's he'd be a great father.

"It's too early to call him now," she said. "But maybe later, okay?"

"Okay," he said in a dejected tone.

Janelle felt bad for him, and toyed with the idea of asking Devon to stop by for a few minutes before work. Not long enough to play a game, but to at least say hi and maybe toss a few baseballs. Maybe he'd even bring his nephew's baseball mitt over.

Warming to the idea, she headed into the kitchen to begin making French toast, deciding to wait until after breakfast to do Sebastian's exchange in order to get him back on a reasonable schedule. From what she could tell, the little boy hadn't suffered any ill effects from the delay in his exchange last night.

Thankfully, no nightmares, either.

Once breakfast was finished and she'd completed Sebastian's exchange, Janelle decided to try calling the teenager, Tina Jamison one more time. The girl hadn't returned her call, which wasn't too encouraging. But it was possible that she'd been busy with homework, or after school activities.

"Oh, yes, I'll get Tina for you," her mother said. "She's off school today and tomorrow."

After a minute a young woman's voice came over the line. "Hello?"

Janelle drew a deep breath and tried to think of the best way to get the girl to agree. "Hi Tina, my name is Janelle Larson and I left your mother a message about possibly doing some babysitting for my son, Sebastian. He has kidney failure and needs peritoneal dialysis exchanges three times a day. Since I knew you recently passed the certified nursing assistant program in Madison, I thought you might be interested in putting some of those patient care skills to good use."

"Oh, yes, my mom just told me you called last night. I would love to help you out, I've recently been accepted into UW Madison starting this fall and I'm hoping to get into the nursing program."

Janelle perked up at this news, even though obviously having Tina babysit was little more than a short term solution. "I love nursing," she confided. "I work in the ER here at Hope County Hospital."

"Really" Tina sounded excited. "I'd love to get a nursing assistant job there for the summer."

"I could give you a reference," Janelle offered, even though she knew that if Tina did get a nursing assistant job she might not have any time to help her out with Sebastian.

"That would be awesome, although I'm sure you'd have to wait and see how well I do with Sebastian first."

Hope bloomed in her chest. "So you'll do it? You'll learn how to do Sebastian's exchanges and maybe watch him on the weekends?"

"Sure, I could even do some evenings if needed," Tina agreed.

Janelle did a quick fist-pump. "Great, thank you so much! I need to work this weekend, is that too soon?"

"Just a minute," Tina said. In the background Janelle heard Tina talking to her mother as they discussed the weekend plans. "I can do Saturday if that helps," Tina said.

"Saturday is perfect. But I'll need you to come over sometime today or tomorrow to learn how to do his exchanges. You're off school, right?"

"Yes, we're off school, but I have plans today. Can I come over tomorrow, instead?"

"Sure." Janelle couldn't believe how things were falling into place at least temporarily. She made plans to meet with Tina tomorrow at one o'clock in the afternoon and then broke the news to Sebastian.

"Tina? Not Mrs. Alice?"

She hesitated, wondering if she should give the retired nurse another chance. "You might need both of them to alternate," she admitted. "I know you don't like Mrs. Alice so I promise I'll keep looking for someone to replace her, okay?"

"Okay," he said, surprising her by his acquiescence. "What happened to my daddy?"

Janelle sucked in a quick breath, unprepared for that question. "I'm not sure," she hedged. "I think he might be sick."

Sebastian's stared at her. "He wasn't very nice to me," he confided. "I was hungry, but he didn't have any food. He kept telling me to shut up and be quiet."

Her heart squeezed in her chest and she quickly crossed over to sit beside him on the sofa. "I'm sorry we argued, Sebastian," she said, hugging him close. "But I want you to know that I love you, very much. I'll never hurt you, but sometimes I will make you do things you don't like to do."

Sebastian burrowed close. "I luv you too, Mommy. And I'm never going to leave you again."

Her eyes went misty with emotion as she pressed a kiss to the top of his head. He'd called her Mommy, again.

She hoped and prayed he'd never stop.

There was a knock at the door, so she regretfully pulled away from Sebastian to answer it. Her pulse jumped when she saw Devon standing on her front porch.

She was a little surprised he wasn't wearing his uniform. He looked so wonderful in a pair of black well-worn jeans and a white button down shirt with the cuffs rolled up, exposing his tanned forearms. It was all she could do not to throw herself into his arms.

"Hi Dev," she greeted him in what she hoped was a casual tone. "Come on, in."

He nodded and stepped over the threshold, glancing over her shoulder at where Sebastian was seated on the sofa. The little boy was playing the racing game, and didn't seem to realize Devon was there. "How is he doing?"

"Pretty well," she informed him. "Do you want to talk to him?"

"If you don't mind."

The hesitancy in his tone made her wince. "Listen, Dev, I'm sorry about last night," she said softly. "It's just that Sebastian idolizes you so much, I'm worried how he's going to handle it when you're gone."

"I know," Devon said, tucking his hands in his back pockets. "Madison offered me a job this morning."

Her stomach sank to the soles of her feet, although she did her best to paste a smile on her face. "That's great news, Devon. I'm so happy for you."

His deep brown gaze searched hers. "I didn't accept the job, yet."

Her mouth dropped open. "You didn't? She echoed in shock. "Why not? I thought that was exactly what you wanted."

He shrugged. "To be honest, another opportunity has come up that I'm considering as well."

Hope deflated quicker than a popped balloon. "Oh, I see. Well, it's good that you're taking your time and considering all your options." She hoped her keen disappointment wasn't too obvious.

"Dev! You came!" Sebastian finally noticed they had

company and slid off the sofa to come running toward Devon. The way Dev picked up her son and held him close made her throat tighten with emotion.

"Did Mommy call you?" Sebastian asked.

Devon glanced at her in surprise. "Uh, no, she didn't. But I do have a couple of questions for you, Sebastian. Do you mind talking to me for a few minutes?"

A tingle of alarm skittered across her nerves. "What do you need to talk to him about?" she asked.

"I'd like to ask him what he remembers from last night," Devon admitted. "It's not my intent to upset him, you can listen in if you like."

Knowing this was a professional visit instead of a personal one stung. But of course she couldn't blame Devon for needing to tie up loose ends from last night, either.

Her problem, if she wanted something more than he was willing to give.

DEVON SEARCHED JANELLE'S FACE, trying to figure out how she felt about his dropping by unexpectedly.

Sheriff Torretti had asked someone else to work his second shift duties, so that he could finish up the investigation against Grant Gardner. In addition, the sheriff had asked him to talk to the Feds about the possibility of collaborating on an anti-drug task force they were creating which was part of the reason he hadn't accepted the job in Madison yet.

The task force sounded intriguing and would span multiple jurisdictions, including their very own Hope County.

But if he were honest with himself, he'd admit that the

real reason he hadn't accepted the Madison job was because of Sebastian and Janelle.

He cared about the boy, but it was Janelle that he couldn't seem to get out of his mind.

Had he imagined the flash of relief in her eyes when he told her he hadn't accepted the Madison job yet?

He forced himself to concentrate on the task at hand, dreading the need to ask Sebastian about what he remembered about last night.

Janelle hovered close, and he didn't blame her. Sebastian admitted that he'd gone along with his daddy when Grant tapped on his window. From there, Sebastian pretty much confirmed their working theory that once Grant had the boy he dragged him out into the woods, claiming they were going camping.

When Sebastian said that his daddy was mean to him, Devon had to work hard not to show his anger. There was nothing he could do about it now, especially considering the fact that Grant would never hurt anyone again.

"Where's my daddy, now?" Sebastian asked. "He's not coming back here, is he?"

"No, your daddy can't come here ever again," Dev assured the boy.

"I don't wanna live wif him," Sebastian persisted, his gaze earnest. "I wanna stay wif my mom."

Dev glanced over at Janelle, who looked as if she might burst into tears any minute. "Sebastian, your daddy is gone forever, so you don't need to worry about him, okay?" He sent a helpless glance at Janelle, unsure of how to tell the boy his father was actually dead.

"He's up in heaven, Sebastian," Janelle spoke up, coming to his rescue.

The boy seemed satisfied with that response. Dev closed his notebook. "That's all I needed, thanks."

"Do you wanna play a game wif me?" Sebastian asked, picking up the controller.

"Dev has to work today, remember?" Janelle said quickly. "Maybe some other time."

"Okay." Sebastian picked up the controller and went back to his racing game.

Devon rose to his feet and headed into the kitchen, hoping to speak to Janelle alone. "Actually, I don't have to report in for my regular shift, Sheriff Torretti gave me some time to finish up the investigation, which included getting Sebastian's statement."

"Oh, I see." She gestured toward the fridge. "Do you want something to drink? I have ice tea or lemonade."

Since she had lemonade on the table, he nodded. "Lemonade would be great, thanks."

When she handed him the glass, he took a sip and then set it down. He felt ridiculously nervous. "Do you have a few minutes to talk?"

She lifted her eyebrow in surprise. "Sure, do you need my statement too?"

"No." He waited until she sat down, then took the seat next to her, so he could take her hand in his. "Janelle, I need to ask you something, and I want you to be completely honest with me, okay?"

She looked a bit apprehensive, but nodded "of course."

He couldn't ever remember feeling this uncertain about a woman. Maybe because he and Debra had known each other for a long time, dated since college. Being with his fiancée had been comfortable, familiar.

Sitting next to Janelle, getting ready to pour his heart and soul out to her, was way outside of his comfort zone. But he wasn't a coward. "Would you consider going out with me?"

She blinked. "You mean, on a date?"

Wasn't it obvious? "Yes, on a date. I don't want to take the job in Madison," he blurted. "I don't want to leave you."

"Me? Or Sebastian?"

"Both of you. I care about Sebastian, but it's you that I keep thinking about." He tightened his grip on her hand. "But if you don't feel the same way, I'll understand."

She looked surprised. "I care about you, too, Devon, but all this time, I thought you were still in love with your fiancée. Wasn't that part of the reason you wanted to move away from here?"

"Not exactly" he knew it was time to tell her the truth. "The Feds want me to help them work on a multi-district task force that would keep me here in Crystal Lake. I wasn't trying to avoid the area, I just wanted to do something important with my life, the way my older brother did."

She didn't look as if she believed him. "I'm sure you have memories of Debra everywhere you look."

He knew it was time to put his past to rest. "I loved Debra, and I was devastated when she was killed. No one knows this, but she was pregnant, just eight weeks along, when she died. And I blamed God for taking her and our child away from me."

"Oh, Dev," she whispered, her eyes full of sympathy. "I'm so sorry for your loss."

"Thank you, but you've shown me the way back to God and my faith. I was wrong to avoid going back to church. But I have to be honest, Janelle. When I realized you had taken custody of Sebastian, I tried to stay away because I couldn't stop thinking about my unborn child a little girl or a boy who would have been close to his age if he or she had lived."

Her gaze was full of compassion. "Those hours that Sebastian was gone were the longest of my entire life. I can't even imagine what you must have gone through."

He was glad she seemed to understand. "Janelle, I didn't intend to open myself up to loving anyone ever again, but somehow, you wiggled your way under my skin and into my heart. I know that it's probably too soon for you to hear this, but I've fallen in love with you. I'm willing to be patient, to give you the time you need to see if you feel the same way."

Janelle's face filled with joy. "Oh, Devon, it's not too soon at all. And I don't need time, I feel the same way. I was so upset about the thought of you moving away from Crystal Lake, I tried to ignore my feelings, but I love you, too. More than I can possibly say."

He surged to his feet, drawing her up and into his arms. "Janelle," he murmured, before leaning down and covering her mouth with his.

She wound her arms around his neck and kissed him back, showing him without words that he wasn't in this alone. Her citrusy scent filled his senses and Devon couldn't believe how blessed he was to have been given a second chance.

A second chance to love and to have a family.

He prolonged the kiss, completely forgetting the fact that they weren't alone until Sebastian interrupted them.

"Why are you kissing Mommy?"

Devon lifted his head, struggling to catch his breath. Janelle hid her face in his shoulder, shaking with repressed laughter.

What kind of question was that? He tried to pull his scrambled brain cells together. "Because I love her," Devon finally responded.

"Me, too," Sebastian agreed.

Dev held his hand out to Sebastian, encouraging him to come over to join them. Using one arm, he lifted the boy up and held him close, keeping his other arm firmly around Janelle.

"Sebastian, I love your mommy very much. How do you feel about us being a family?"

Janelle's face broke into a wide smile, and she put her arm around Sebastian, including him in the three-way hug.

"Would we live together like a real family?" Sebastian asked.

Devon nodded. "I'd be your new daddy," he added "if that's okay with you."

"Yay!" Sebastian cried out. "God answered my prayers!"

Devon tightened his grip on Janelle and Sebastian, knowing that God had answered his prayers, too.

EPILOGUE

Janelle stood in the back of the church, smoothing a hand over her white gown as she waited for Lexi Ryerson, Julie and Derek's daughter, and Sebastian to walk down the aisle. They looked so cute, even though Lexi hadn't wanted anything to do with holding Sebastian's hand.

When Sebastian reached the front of the church, Devon stepped forward to take the wedding rings from the little boy, then he drew Sebastian to his side, where he would participate in their wedding ceremony.

The music swelled, and Janelle stepped forward to make her way down the aisle. Devon's dark gaze captured hers, admiration and happiness shining from his eyes.

She smiled, anxious to begin a new life with Devon. The past few months had passed in a whirlwind of wedding plans, since neither one of them had wanted a long engagement.

Janelle was so thankful the Lord had brought them together, and with their friends and the Crystal Lake townsfolk watching, they'd vow to love and honor each other for the rest of their lives.

Devon couldn't wait, but stepped forward to take her hand in his. She let him draw her up to the front of the church where Pastor John waited for them.

The ceremony was sweetly poignant. "This ring is a sign of my love and fidelity, for as long as we both shall live," Devon murmured, slipping her wedding band on the third finger of her left hand.

She took his ring, and repeated the vow to him. "This ring is a sign of my love and fidelity, for as long as we both shall live."

Pastor John's grin was broad as he lifted his hands to encompass the crowd packed into the church. "I know pronounce you husband and wife. Please welcome Devon and Janelle Armbruster."

The crowd broke into wild applause, and Devon bent his head to give her a firm kiss. "I love you, Mrs. Armbruster," he whispered.

"I love you, too, Deputy Armbruster," she replied. She placed her hand in the crook of Devon's arm, then she grasped Sebastian's hand so the three of them could walk down the aisle, together. They made their way to the back of the church, where everyone would gather for their reception.

"Are you ready for your wedding present?" Devon asked in a low tone as they took their place in the receiving line.

She glanced at him in surprise. "A present? But I didn't get you anything," she protested.

Devon grinned. "This present is for our family. I didn't want to say anything until I knew for sure, but I had my blood and tissue testing done to see if I'm a potential match for Sebastian. Turns out, my blood type is O negative. I've been approved to donate a kidney for our son."

"What?" Janelle could hardly believe what he was saying. "Are you sure?"

"Yes, the doctors assured me that my kidney would absolutely work for Sebastian. We can schedule the surgery any time."

"Oh, Devon, that's amazing news, but are you absolutely sure you want to do this?" Janelle was surprised and humbled by his willingness to donate a kidney for Sebastian. "This isn't something to take lightly, there are risks. Not just surgical risks, but the risk of you suffering kidney failure later in life."

"I know, the transplant surgeon explained everything to me, and I know there's a possibility I'll have more complications as I get older, but Janelle, it's worth the risk to provide Sebastian a healthy life." He stared down at her intently. "You would do this for our son if you were a match, so why shouldn't I?"

She didn't have an argument for that one, so she simply threw her arms around his neck and kissed him again. "I love you so much," she whispered.

"I love you, too," he whispered back.

Janelle was forced to release him when the wedding guests filed out of the church and lined up to wish them well.

As she thanked everyone for coming, she knew deep in her heart that everything would work out fine, because she and Devon loved each other.

There was no doubt God was watching over them.

Dear Reader,

I hope you enjoyed *Second Chance*, the sixth book in my Crystal Lake Series. Many readers have been asking for Deputy Devon Armbruster's story, so I decided to give him a second chance at love and faith. As a critical care nurse, I also worked with transplant recipients so I decided to give the story a bit of a twist with ER nurse Janelle's nephew, Sebastian, requiring peritoneal dialysis and hopefully one day being given the gift of life with a kidney transplant. And of course, there is nothing better than falling in love and becoming a family.

If you would be so kind as to leave a review from the site where you purchased this book, I'd greatly appreciate it.

I love hearing from my readers. You can write to me and sign up for my newsletter through my website at www.laurascottbooks.com. I only send newsletters to announce new releases and I do offer a free exclusive Crystal Lake Novella for all subscribers. Or find me on Facebook at Laura Scott Books Author, and on Twitter @laurascottbooks.

Yours in faith,

Laura Scott

PS If you like reading my books I've included a sneak peak of the first chapter of my new Series The McNallys.

TO LOVE - THE MCNALLYS

Several loud thuds brought Jazzlyn McAndrew up from a sound sleep. For a minute, she thought the noise had been something she'd dreamed, then she heard it again. Louder. She wasn't sure, but it almost sounded as if several two-by-fours were being dropped.

What in the world?

She rolled out of bed, tugging her oversized T-shirt down over her gym shorts and headed downstairs, wincing as the wooden board creaked beneath her bare feet. What if the noise was from somewhere inside the house? She reached the bottom of the stairs, she flattened herself against the wall, then gingerly peered around the corner, looking into the great room.

Casting her gaze over the main living area, the fireplace, the light house oil painting over the mantle and the antique glossy cherry wood furniture, nothing seemed out of place. But she knew she hadn't imagined the sounds, so as she made her way through her grandparents' old mansion she picked up a claw hammer, to use as a possible weapon.

Everything was fine inside the house, but when she

walked over to the French doors overlooking Lake Michigan, she noticed several boards strewn across the lawn.

Her repaired gazebo!

Sick to her stomach, Jazz flung open the doors and stumbled outside.

No! It couldn't be! Two sections of the gazebo she'd worked on for the past three days had been destroyed in one fell swoop. She stared in horror, her mind trying to comprehend what had happened. Vandals had struck, in fact the sledge hammer they'd used was still lying in the center of the destruction.

But who would do such a thing? And why?

In the early morning light, she could see the area was deserted. Whoever had done this was long gone. Maybe in the time it took her to go through the house. It was difficult to tear her gaze away from the damaged remnants of her hard work.

She shivered in the crisp April breeze coming off the lake. Drawing a deep shuddering breath, she turned and went back inside to find her cell phone. She called the Clark County Sheriff's deputy for the second time in a week.

The first incident, a broken window in the front door had been bad enough.

But this? Destroying two sections of the gazebo she'd recently repaired? This time, the vandals had gone too far.

"Clark County Sheriff's department," the female dispatcher answered. "How can I help you?"

"This is Jazzlyn McAndrew and I need a deputy here ASAP. The vandals have used my sledge hammer to wreck my gazebo, it's lying in pieces across my lawn."

"I'll send a deputy," the dispatcher responded. The

woman didn't ask for her address, the entire town knew where the McAndrew mansion was located.

"Thank you." Jazz disconnected from the call and combed her fingers through her disheveled hair, her inner fury subsiding to a dull resignation. Even if the police found who'd done this, she would still need to fix everything that had been destroyed. At this rate, her goal of opening the B&B before Memorial Day wasn't going to happen.

She gave herself a mental shake, knowing she needed to remain positive. She could do this. How much time before the deputy arrived? She figured she had ten minutes at the most, so she ran upstairs to the green room she'd been using to change into a sweatshirt and jeans.

The green room was her favorite, the one she'd always stayed in when visiting.

Five minutes later, Jazz returned to the kitchen to brew a pot of coffee. The scent helped her to relax a bit, and she poured a cup, grateful for the jolt of caffeine.

But when the deputy still hadn't arrived by the time she'd finished two cups of coffee, her anger began to simmer. By eight o'clock in the morning, she tapped her foot on the floor, wondering how long it would take for someone to arrive.

Apparently, vandalism of personal property wasn't high on the Clark County Sheriff's list of priorities.

Another hour passed. A knock at the front door made her frown. She hadn't heard a car come up the driveway. Setting her coffee aside, she reached for her claw hammer, and made her way to the newly repaired front door. She peeked through the recently replaced window.

A man roughly six feet tall with longish dark hair stood there, wearing a threadbare red and gray checkered flannel shirt, faded black jeans and construction boots.

Not the deputy.

The vandal? But why knock at her door?

She hesitated so long he rapped again, a little louder this time. The stranger hunched his shoulders and rubbed his hands together as if he were cold. No car meant he'd either walked or hitch-hiked from town.

Against her better judgement, she opened the door still holding the claw hammer in clear view as she eyed him with suspicion. "Yes?"

The stranger smiled, but it didn't reach his dark eyes. "Ms. McAndrew? My name is Dalton O'Brien and I was told by Stuart Sewell from the hardware store that you might be looking for some construction help. I work hard and accept cash if you're interested."

Jazz stared at him for a long moment, wondering if this guy was really brazen enough to destroy her gazebo then come back to ask to be paid to fix it. "How did you get here?"

He looked surprised at her question. "I hitched a ride from the Pine Cone Campsite, the driver let me out on Main Street so I walked from there."

The Pine Cone Campsite was over twenty miles from the center of town. If he was being honest, then he probably wasn't her vandal.

Still, she didn't like the timing of his arrival.

"I can provide references if needed," O'Brien went on. "I did some work on Mrs. Cromwell's bathroom a week ago."

Jazz knew Betty Cromwell. Everyone in town knew Betty, the woman was one of the biggest sources of gossip in McAndrew Bay. If Betty would vouch for this guy, she may be interested.

She was just about to ask for his contact information when a dark brown sedan pulled in the words Clark County Sheriff's Department etched along the side. Finally!

Dalton O'Brien turned to watch the cop car approach, not looking the least bit nervous as he tucked his hands into the front pockets of his jeans.

Trusting her instincts wasn't easy. Jazz had learned the hard way that she was too naïve when it came to trusting men. Yet for some reason, she didn't think the handsome stranger was the person who'd vandalized her gazebo.

Or maybe she just didn't want to believe it.

"Ma'am, I'm Deputy Garth Lewis. I understand you've had more trouble this morning?"

"Yes." Jazz opened the door wider and gestured with her hand. "Come in, both of you. I have fresh coffee if you're interested."

Both Dalton and Deputy Lewis glanced around with interest. While she loved the beautiful great room, she led the way into the kitchen and pulled two coffee mugs out of the cabinet.

"O'Brien," Deputy Lewis said with a nod. "Are you here, looking for work?"

"Yes sir." Dalton didn't say anything more, and the two men stood awkwardly in the large kitchen.

It was reassuring that the deputy knew Dalton O'Brien by name. She handed them both steaming mugs of coffee. "Cream or sugar?"

"Black is fine," Deputy Lewis said.

"For me, too," Dalton added.

"Okay then. Mr. O'Brien, why don't you have a seat for a moment while I talk to the deputy?" She crossed over to the French doors, opened them and then stepped back so the Deputy could see the vandalism for himself.

Deputy Lewis let out a low whistle. "When did this happen?"

She crossed her arms over her Michigan State sweatshirt. "The noise woke me up at six this morning. I went through the house first, so I didn't see the damage out here right away. By the time I did whoever had done this was long gone."

The deputy met her gaze. "I saw your report about the damaged front door, and now this. Do you have any enemies that we need to know about?"

"None that I'm aware of." Jazz glanced at the stranger who'd come over to see the vandalism for himself. Then she turned back to the deputy. "You probably know this house belonged to my grandparents, Jerry and Joan McAndrew. Our family has lived here in Clark County for a hundred and fifty years, since our great-great grandparents immigrated from Ireland. The bay was named after them."

"I'm well aware of the town history," Deputy Lewis said in a dry tone.

She gestured to the interior of the large Victorian house that she was in the process of turning into McAndrews B&B. "My siblings and I only spent summers here, until our grandma passed away, willing the property to us. You'd know more about any possible enemies than I would."

"What's the approximate cost of the damage?" Deputy Lewis asked as he pulled out a small notepad and stubby pencil.

"Around two grand," the stranger said. "Maybe less, depending on how much of the lumber can be salvaged."

She stared at him in surprise. "That's exactly what I would have estimated," she murmured. "I guess you know your way around construction sites."

O'Brien gave a curt nod. "I do."

"Well then." Jazz let out her breath in a heavy sigh. "I guess I could use a little help, if you're willing."

The stranger nodded and took another sip of his coffee.

Jazz waited for Deputy Lewis to finish his report, which included taking pictures of the crime scene. He also bagged the sledge hammer, on the off chance he might be able to lift some fingerprints from the wooden handle. The deputy left, promising to be in touch if he had any news. Afterwards, she returned to the kitchen, the stranger following like her shadow.

"You hungry?" she asked.

His eyes flared with hope. "Yes, Ma'am."

"Please call me Jazz, Ma'am makes me feel old. Veggie omelets okay?"

"I'm not picky," he said in a wry tone.

"Good." Jazz opened the fridge and pulled out a carton of eggs and the veggies—broccoli, onions and mushrooms that were left over from the night before. "After breakfast, we'll get to work."

He nodded again without saying anything more.

A man of few words, she thought, his dark eyes shadowed with secrets. She told herself it didn't matter why he was hitching rides and living in a campsite. Not her business one way or the other.

Jazz only needed his assistance for the next couple of weeks, then he could be on his way. Fine with her, because she didn't need any complications in her life.

Or distractions.

In Dalton's opinion, the veggie omelet Jazz had made for him, was the best he'd ever tasted, but as usual, he kept his thoughts to himself.

He was only here to make a few extra bucks before moving on. His plan was to head further north, knowing that construction jobs would be plentiful there during the summer months.

The damage to the gazebo made him mad, especially the way Jazz had looked so devastated at the senseless destruction.

Ms. McAndrew, he sternly reminded himself. Okay, yeah, she was beautiful with her long dark brown hair tousled from sleep, and her petite, curvy figure. The way she'd answered the door holding a claw hammer had made him smile, the image still burned into his memory. Beauty aside, he had no intention of crossing the line between employer and employee.

He was a drifter. As soon as this job was finished, he'd be on his way.

Truthfully, he was happy to help. He hated the idea of a young woman living in this huge rambling house alone, while vandals went to town on her gazebo.

It wasn't right. He didn't know anything about the McAndrew legacy, since he'd only been in town for a couple of weeks now, but he had to agree with the deputy that the culprit must be someone holding a grudge against the family.

Which meant just about anyone in town could be considered a possible suspect.

Dalton finished his second cup of coffee, then carried his dirty dishes to the sink. "Thanks for breakfast," he said, then headed outside to see what he could salvage from the wreckage.

Not expecting to be put to work right away, Dalton had left his tool belt at the Pine Cone Campsite. He considered asking Jazz to drive him over there, then figured she probably had enough tools here for him to use.

By the time Jazz joined him, he'd picked through the entire pile. The lumber he'd stacked together on the right side of the gazebo was good enough to be used again, the left side held the lumber split beyond repair.

"That's better than I'd hoped, this could come in closer to a thousand to repair, excluding labor."

"Agreed. If you're willing loan me tools I'll begin construction."

"I don't have extras," Jazz said, her expression full of apology. "But you can use anything I have while I head out to buy more lumber."

"Or, if you don't mind swinging past the Pine Cone Campsite, I can pick up my tools," he offered. "We can get the lumber on the way back. With both of us working, we'll get this repaired in no time."

For the first time since he'd arrived, she broke into a wide smile. "Let's do it."

She was alarmingly stunning when she smiled, and he had to force himself to turn away. What was wrong with him? His wife Debbie and their young son, Davy have only been gone eleven months, not even a full year. He wasn't about to try replacing them in his heart.

Not now. Not ever.

He followed Jazz through the old Victorian house to the circle drive out front. He hadn't paid much attention to the three-car garage, painted yellow with white trim to match the large house, but that's where Jazz headed.

Pushing numbers into a key pad, she stood and waited for the garage door to open. He wasn't sure why he expected to see a small compact car, instead of the large bright blue Chevy pick-up truck.

"Nice," he said, his tone full of appreciation. As soon as the words left his lips, he frowned. He didn't need a truck, or any other flashy items. That was part of a life he'd left behind and had no interest in returning to. All he needed was a tent, backpack, sleeping bag, and his tools.

"Thanks." Jazz didn't seem to notice anything amiss. She waited till he was seated beside her, before heading out of the garage, closing the door with the push of a button.

The ride to the campground didn't take long. Jazz followed his directions as he told her where to find his camping spot. The red tent was right where he'd left it. He slid out of the passenger seat and went over to unzip the front flap. His backpack, camping gear and tools were tucked inside.

He emerged a few minutes later to find Jazz standing in front of his tent, regarding it thoughtfully. He lifted his construction tool belt. "I'm ready."

She nodded absently. "Do they charge you a fee to camp here?"

"Yeah, but it's nominal. Why?"

She bit her lower lip for a moment. "How would you feel about camping outside my place, instead? It's free and I'll throw in meals."

He shouldn't have been surprised, but he was. His first instinct was to refuse, he liked her too much already. But then he remembered the vandalism.

It wasn't his problem to keep her property safe. She'd notified the cops who would probably keep a close eye on things. Then again, he knew the deputies couldn't be there all the time. And if the vandals lived in town, they could be at the old Victorian and back within an hour.

"Never mind," Jazz said hastily, as if sensing his reluctance. "It's a crazy idea."

Yeah, it was, but he nodded anyway. "I'll do it."

Her blue eyes widened in surprise. "You will?"

"Yes. Although we haven't agreed on an hourly wage yet."

She named a fair sum, better than he'd hoped considering she was offering meals, too.

He took a step toward her and held out his hand. "Thank you. I'll take it."

She placed her small, yet slightly calloused hand in his, sending a sliver of awareness down his spine. He did his best to ignore it as they solemnly shook.

"It's a deal." She smiled again, stealing his breath. "I'll help you pack."

"No need, I have a system." He dropped her hand and stepped back, needing distance. He went to work dismantling his campsite with the ease of long practice.

After storing his items in the space behind the bench seat, he climbed in beside her, hoping he wasn't making a huge mistake.

Made in the USA
Monee, IL
12 January 2023

25128523R00111